Embroidery Bee

De-ann Black

Paperback edition published 2025

Embroidery Bee

ISBN: 9798309870219

Cover embroidery by De-ann Black.

De-ann's embroidery pattern books are on Amazon:

Floral Garden Embroidery Patterns
Christmas & Winter Embroidery Patterns
Floral Spring Embroidery Patterns
Sea Theme Embroidery Patterns

Embroidery Bee is the first book in a new romance series.

Also by De-ann Black (Romance, Action/Thrillers & Children's books). See her Amazon Author page or website for further details about her books, screenplays, illustrations and artwork. www.De-annBlack.com

Romance:
Crafting Bee
Scottish Highlands New Year Ball
Ballroom Dancing Christmas Romance
Christmas Ballroom Dancing
Autumn Romance
Knitting & Starlight
Knitting Bee
The Sweetest Waltz
Sweet Music
Love & Lyrics
Christmas Weddings
Fairytale Christmas on the Island
The Cure for Love at Christmas
Vintage Dress Shop on the Island
Scottish Island Fairytale Castle
Scottish Loch Summer Romance
Scottish Island Knitting Bee
Sewing & Mending Cottage
Knitting Shop by the Sea
Colouring Book Cottage
Knitting Cottage
Oops! I'm the Paparazzi, Again
The Bitch-Proof Wedding
Embroidery Cottage
The Dressmaker's Cottage
The Sewing Shop
Heather Park
The Tea Shop by the Sea
The Bookshop by the Seaside
The Sewing Bee

The Quilting Bee
Snow Bells Wedding
Snow Bells Christmas
Summer Sewing Bee
The Chocolatier's Cottage
Christmas Cake Chateau
The Beemaster's Cottage
The Sewing Bee By The Sea
The Flower Hunter's Cottage
The Christmas Knitting Bee
The Sewing Bee & Afternoon Tea
Shed In The City
The Bakery By The Seaside
The Christmas Chocolatier
The Christmas Tea Shop & Bakery
The Bitch-Proof Suit

Action/Thrillers:

Knight in Miami.   Electric Shadows.
Agency Agenda.   The Strife of Riley.
Love Him Forever.   Shadows of Murder.
Someone Worse.

Colouring books:

Summer Nature. Flower Nature. Summer Garden. Spring
Garden. Autumn Garden. Sea Dream. Festive Christmas.
Christmas Garden. Flower Bee. Wild Garden. Flower
Hunter. Stargazer Space. Christmas Theme. Faerie Garden
Spring. Scottish Garden Seasons. Bee Garden.

Embroidery books:

Floral Garden Embroidery Patterns
Floral Spring Embroidery Patterns
Christmas & Winter Embroidery Patterns
Floral Nature Embroidery Designs
Scottish Garden Embroidery Designs

Contents

CHAPTER ONE

The turquoise sea sparkled in the morning light, and Leith shielded his eyes to gaze out at the beautiful Scottish Highlands coastline. Perched on a ladder, mending the roof of one of the traditional cottages dotted along the edge of the quaint village, he saw no hint of a storm. He'd woken up in the depths of the night feeling that a storm was brewing. Brought up in the seaside village, his senses were never wrong. And yet...

Shades of turquoise water, crested with a few white frothy waves washed gently towards the white sand, and faded into the distance, far away to the hazy outline of the distant islands.

Situated far north on the west coast of Scotland, the village was tucked into a niche in the picturesque landscape that on bright summer days like this, with a vast azure sky arching above it, looked like a continental paradise.

The summer had arrived early, merging seamlessly with the mild spring, encouraging him to discard his jumper, and work in the white T–shirt and jeans that showed his broad shoulders, lean–muscled arms and taut physique. At six foot plus, thirty–two, and with a rugged handsomeness, he was a fine figure of a man. His ruffled auburn hair would soon start to lighten to a fiery gold from another summer outdoors. But this year, he had well–laid plans that no storm was sweeping off course. Not this time.

Leith pulled his pale blue gaze away from the sea, kept a grip of his hammer in his sturdy work gloves, and continued to mend his cottage roof. A minor repair that his years of building work experience handled efficiently.

He'd almost finished when he noticed a familiar figure approaching from further along the grassy shore.

Donal raised his hand to wave to Leith. Fit and in his fifties, Donal managed the local castle's estate. He had news that he knew would rattle Leith's world to the core. But the lad needed to know what was coming.

As he reached the cottage, Donal's usual cheery expression was dour.

Leith looked down at him from the ladder. 'Is there something wrong?'

'I've got news.'

Leith steeled himself. Maybe a storm was incoming.

'Ionna is coming back.' Donal's words shattered Leith's day into a hundred uneasy shards.

Leith had been right. A storm that would sweep his world at a tilt was heading his way. Not the type he could coorie in and shelter from in his cottage. This was an assault on his heart. No. Holds. Barred.

'Does the laird know?' Leith kept his voice steady, but underneath the gloves his knuckles were white with the tense grip he had on the hammer and the edge of the ladder.

'Not yet. I'm on my way to the castle. But I thought I'd tell you first.'

Leith nodded acknowledgement of this.

'Her Aunty Effy told me that Ionna's coming for a visit when I handed in a parcel this morning.' Donal often picked up parcels that were delivered to the village's wee shop and took them up to the castle. Seeing a parcel for Effy, he'd dropped it off at her cottage on his way, rightly assuming it was embroidery thread, yarn and other items for her crafting.

Ionna was raised by Effy after she lost her mother when she was still at school. Her father had never been on the scene for long, and Ionna had no memories of him. It had always been Ionna and her mother, then just her and Effy and the local ladies that rallied round. A shared love of crafts and skills, particularly embroidery, had been passed on to Ionna since she was a wee girl.

Ionna had grown up to become an expert in embroidery work, designing her own patterns. Eventually, a series of unwise choices led to Ionna leaving the village for a new and exciting life in Edinburgh on the other side of Scotland. Burning connections with those in the local community she'd once been close to. Barely exchanging birthday and Christmas cards with Effy. Rare phone calls at first that dwindled to none at all. Until recently.

'Bridges mended?' said Leith.

'Patched. Temporarily.'

Leith held in the tense breath that threatened to escape and reveal how hard the news had hit him.

Donal forced a resigned smile and then went on his way.

Watching him walk across the rough grass towards the forest, Leith fought the urge to find out more details. And lost. Climbing down the ladder, throwing the hammer into his canvas work bag, he ran after him.

'Donal!' he called out.

Glancing round, Donal waited as Leith caught up.

'Is it just a quick visit?' Leith's heart pounded like the hammer he'd been using.

'Effy has agreed that Ionna can come and stay with her at the cottage for a wee while.'

'How long?' The tension in Leith's tone was evident.

'A season.'

'The whole summer!' Leith's voice resonated through the quietude.

Roary heard raised voices as he ran through the forest on one of his daily runs. Dressed head to toe in black fitness gear, including black training shoes, he recognised Donal's voice and changed his route to head towards the ruckus.

Roary's hair was as dark as the shadows in the depths of the trees and his eyes were an intense forest green, one of his outstanding features in an already handsome face. The laird was the same age and height as Leith. The only things they had in common, apart from a turbulent past entwined with Ionna.

'Don't wind yourself up into a lather,' Donal told Leith.

Taking a deep breath, Leith calmed down. An entire summer with Ionna in their midst hadn't been included in his plans.

Donal revealed Ionna's plan. 'Ionna phoned her aunty out of the blue last week, testing to see if the welcome mat would be pulled out from under her feet if she dared to set foot in the village again.'

'And?'

'Ionna is working on one of her new embroidery pattern books. The publishers are snapping at her to get a shifty on. She has a deadline, and...apparently when she split with her boyfriend, things went awry. Her fancy flat in Edinburgh is expensive. In a nutshell, she's made a mess of things. So she's coming here to finish the book. Effy will sort her out.'

Effy could sort most people out, and didn't suffer any nonsense from anyone. But Leith wasn't sure she could tame the troublemaking spark in Ionna.

'Ionna is...unintentionally, a troublemaker.'

'And the sky's blue.' Donal smiled. 'Effy and Ionna are the only family each other have these days.'

She could've had a life with him, built their own wee family together. Leith pressed his lips into a firm line to prevent himself venting on what might have been if she'd loved him instead of the laird.

Roary kept running.

A forest of pines watched the village's back. It shielded the local castle, hidden in the depths of the forest, surrounded on all sides. As the castle's laird, Roary, a single man by circumstances rather than choice, valued his privacy.

Residing in a hidden castle suited him perfectly, even though his life was less than ideal. The past few years, he'd felt the urge to find the right woman and settle down. But the laird's notorious untamed streak was managing to forgo what wasn't presently attainable.

Instead, he was looking forward to an early summer where he could enjoy the benefits of living by the sea and the countryside, away from the hustle and bustle of the cities he was required to visit on business several times a year. His business trips, dealing with investments, helped to keep the castle and its estate solvent. He'd only just returned from a trip to London. The forecast promised a gorgeous early summer. A scorcher. So any further business and hopes of romance could wait until the autumn and winter. Or whenever the woman of his dreams walked into his life, and into his castle.

Bursting through a gap in the trees, Roary ran into the grassy clearing, still hearing the voices, and now seeing in the near distance Donal talking to Leith. His estate manager and the local builder got along well, but he sensed tension in the fresh sea air blowing in from the shore.

Leith saw Roary running towards them. His reaction caused Donal to glance round. Friction sparked whenever the laird and Leith were forced to talk to each other, which was hardly ever these days.

'I heard voices,' Roary called to them, barely out of breath as he approached and stopped to join the conversation. 'Is there something going on?' Clearly, there was.

Donal didn't sugar the pill. 'Ionna is coming back to visit Effy.'

In one sentence, Roary joined the dots regarding the tension.

'I'm busy that day.' Roary's deep voice made his intentions evident.

'It's not a flying visit. She's here for the summer,' Donal added.

Roary ran a hand through his thick dark hair pushing it back from his pale features. 'I was looking forward to a nice relaxing summer.' The green eyes looked at Leith for comment on the situation.

'I've only just found out. My plans won't change. I'm going to finish working on my cottage during the summer. The exterior is nearly done. I've only the interior to redecorate and the garden to tend. And another couple of cottages to restore. I'm not having my plans derailed because of Ionna.'

Roary sighed heavily. His summer had the shine taken off it.

Leith sensed his ire. 'Since when did you ever let a lassie throw you off your stride?'

'She threw you off yours years ago,' Roary retorted. 'I bet you've still got the battle scars.'

Leith let the jibe slide off his broad shoulders. He looked at Donal. 'When is she due to arrive?'

'Later today,' said Donal. 'Ionna phoned Effy at the crack of dawn this morning to say she was leaving Edinburgh and driving here.'

Leith scoffed. 'We'll expect her next Tuesday.'

Donal tried not to smile. 'She should arrive sometime this afternoon, probably.'

The three men shared a knowing look.

Leith shook his head in dismay. 'Ionna could get herself lost in an empty house, never mind drive from Edinburgh, across to the west coast, and then all the way up to the village in the Highlands.'

No argument from the laird and Donal.

Realising there was no more to be said on the matter, Roary ran back into the forest leaving the problem dangling in the sea air.

Effy's cottage was further along the coast from Leith with a beautiful sea view from the front windows. One of several whitewashed cottages scattered like sweeties, she was only a two–minute walk from the little main street where a selection of pretty shops and small businesses thrived.

Effy was in her fifties, trim, wearing an apron over her cotton dress, and her barley blonde hair was pinned up in a tidy chignon. A widow, with no children of her own, she'd been happy to bring up her sister's wee girl.

A garden surrounded the cottage, and Effy stepped out of her kitchen into the back garden, wearing her comfy slippers, to take her washing in. The white linen sheets and pillowcases had dried nicely in the mild sea breeze.

'It's a fine day for drying a washing, Effy,' one of the local crafting bee ladies called to her. Vaila was on her way to the wee shop for groceries. She'd gone to school with Ionna in the nearest small town. Vaila, thirty, had dark chestnut hair that framed her alabaster complexion, and modelled part–time to supplement her crafting earnings. 'Getting everything ready for Ionna's arrival?'

Effy folded the bed linen and put it in her wash basket while she chatted to Vaila. 'Yes, I've prepared the spare bedroom for her.' Effy would've had it ready sooner, but she'd waited to see if Ionna was really going to come to the village. The morning phone call confirmed she was on her way, so Effy dealt with the last piece of the rearranging of her home to accommodate her niece.

The pillowcases were a set she'd embroidered at the edges with flowers. She'd unlisted the quilt she'd recently finished that was for sale on her crafting website. It was due to be used on Ionna's bed. A personal, beautiful and handcrafted welcome home.

'I've made a pot of broth,' said Effy. 'Something easy to heat up when she arrives.' Whenever that would be. Between now and midnight.

'Are you still holding the embroidery bee in your cottage this evening?'

'Oh, yes. No change to our schedule. Ionna will have to fit in with our world.'

'I'm glad because a few of us were thinking that...well, now Ionna's coming back that there could be a...' Vaila searched for a tactful phrase.

Effy put it bluntly before Vaila could find one. 'A stooshie.'

Vaila tried to smile as Effy suggested a rumpus. 'It's just that, we all know what Ionna is like. Or at least how she used to be.'

'All hoity–toity!' Another woman spoke up, overhearing their conversation and joining in on her way to the main street. Mairead was similar in age to Effy, wore her light brown hair in a bun, and was a member of the crafting bee.

Effy folded the pillowcases and put them on top of the sheets. 'I won't be putting up with any of her nonsense. You know me well enough to understand that.'

'But why is she coming back here, after all these years?' said Mairead. 'Doesn't she have a posh flat in Edinburgh?'

'She did,' said Effy. 'Then the rent became too expensive, so she gave it up.'

'Couldn't she have found a cheaper flat to rent in Edinburgh?' Mairead suggested.

Effy exhaled deeply. 'That would've been the sensible thing to do.'

The women exchanged a resigned look.

'I thought she had a well–to–do boyfriend?' said Vaila.

'He dumped her recently,' Effy revealed. 'She thought he was going to propose, but instead he said that he was still in love with his Irish ex–girlfriend, Tara, and was getting engaged to her.'

Mairead frowned. 'That must've stung.'

'Ionna's better off without that sort of man,' said Vaila.

'She is, but she needs time to relax, get herself and her personal life unfankled, everything sorted out,' said Effy. 'Unfortunately she doesn't have that, because her publishers want her to create another embroidery book. She's on a fairly tight deadline. So, she's coming here, to stay with me and work on finishing her book. Away from the city, away from all the trouble she's stirred up for herself.'

'And bringing it here to your doorstep, Effy.' Mairead was concerned for her friend.

Effy sounded determined. 'I'll sort her out.'

They didn't doubt it.

'What about Leith?' Mairead glanced along the coast towards his cottage. 'Does he know yet?'

'Aye, Donal told him this morning,' Effy confirmed.

'How did he take the news?' said Mairead.

Effy shrugged. 'Donal gave me a quick call to say he'd told Leith and the laird.'

'Neither of them will be happy, unless Leith still holds a candle for her,' Vaila suggested.

'It was a long time ago,' said Effy. 'He's a grown man with his own life.'

'Leith has never settled down,' Mairead remarked. 'Some folk say he never got over her leaving the village.'

'Ionna never dated Leith,' Effy stated clearly. 'We all know he loved her, but she only had eyes for Roary, and the laird had no interest in her.'

'It was a squinty love triangle with all the wrong angles,' Mairead assessed.

'What about the laird?' said Vaila. 'Does Ionna still fancy him?'

Effy sounded defensive of her niece. 'No. She was just a young lassie with a crush on the laird. Just like a lot of lassies.' Effy directed her remark straight at Vaila. 'Dreaming of being like a fairytale princess in his beautiful castle.'

11

Vaila tried not to blush.

'Roary's never settled down either,' Mairead added.

'He's dated models that he's met on his trips to the cities.' Vaila relayed the gossip she'd heard.

'Did Ionna see Roary on the front cover of that magazine?' said Mairead. 'He's even more handsome than when she left.'

Roary was sometimes interviewed by the press and appeared in media news regarding him being the laird of a castle in the Scottish Highlands.

'No, I don't think so,' said Effy. 'Ionna doesn't talk about Roary. She made a new life for herself in Edinburgh. Her embroidery books are a success. Her personal life is a mess. She's made it clear that she's putting romance on the back burner to concentrate on her latest embroidery book.'

'Do you think she'll stay longer than the summer? Move back to the village?' said Vaila.

Effy shook her head. 'No. I don't think that Ionna will stay.' There was a hint of sadness in Effy's tone.

'I'm sorry you're having your plans for the summer ruined, Effy,' said Mairead.

Effy took a deep breath. 'I'd planned to travel and see lots of places in Scotland that I'd never visited. Those towns and cities will still be there after Ionna has left. They'll be less busy in the autumn, less expensive, and I'll go gadding about then.'

Effy picked up her wash basket. 'I'll see the two of you tonight, as usual. I had a delivery of a new range of embroidery thread and crewel wool. You'll love the latest colours.'

Smiling, the women continued on to the shops, and Effy carried her washing inside, glancing back along the coast to Leith's cottage.

The late afternoon sun glinted off the surface of the sea, dazzling Leith as he worked in his garden. He hadn't stopped for lunch, hoping the hard work would quell his troubled heart. No luck yet.

The bramble hedging needed trimmed, so he started work on that until grey clouds cast a shadow across the coast, shielding out the sunlight in the garden.

Leith sensed a storm was coming, not rain or thunder, but a beautiful whirlwind of trouble.

Shivering in the fading light, he saw Donal approaching from the forest where he'd been working on the castle's estate. Aware that the time was wearing on, he headed towards Leith with the latest news on Ionna's arrival.

'She's not here yet,' said Donal, stopping at the edge of the garden where Leith had trimmed the bramble hedging and tamed the climbing roses that scrambled over the archway, taking a wild route along the front of the cottage.

Leith dug his spade into the ground and took a breather from digging up part of the flower beds that were becoming overcrowded.

'I called Effy,' Donal continued. 'No word of Ionna's whereabouts. Effy doesn't want to phone her when she's driving.'

'What local route is she taking?'

Donal tried not to smirk. 'The roundabout one I presume.'

Leith felt the muscles in his face relax into a smile having been tense for the past few hours.

'Did Effy tell her not to take the old route down through the forest?' said Leith. 'The stream makes it bogged down these days. She'll get mired in the mud. Her car will get stuck in the glaur.'

'Yes.'

'Did she listen?'

'Anybody's guess.'

A message came through on Donal's phone from Effy. He read it and shook his head at Leith. 'Ionna didnae listen.'

Leith took his gardening gloves off, cast them down on the freshly mown lawn and gave Donal a knowing look.

'I'll get the tractor ready.' Donal sighed and started to walk away towards one of the estate's fields.

Leith followed him, muttering. 'And so it begins...'

CHAPTER TWO

Leith and Donal chatted as they walked across the field to get one of the tractors. Topic of conversation — Ionna.

'She'll be thirty now,' Leith said thoughtfully. Two years younger than him. Twice as troublesome, foolhardy and adventurous. Take your pick. Whatever way the wind was blowing. As changeable as the local weather. Three seasons in a single day — bright and sunny, cold and rainy, or blaw the hat aff yer heid blustery.

Donal hadn't calculated her age. He glanced at Leith.

'It was her birthday last week,' Leith explained.

Donal gave him a look.

'It's an easy date to remember.'

The needle of truth pointed more towards him never forgetting her birthday.

'She must've been twenty–four when she left the village,' Donal calculated. 'Six years? I wonder what she's like these days? She was always a beauty. A heartbreaker.' Donal bit his lip. 'Sorry.'

Leith shrugged this truth aside.

'What are you going to do about her coming here?' Donal's words were filled with concern.

'Get on with my building work. As I said to the laird, I'm not changing my plans for the summer. The cottages need renovated on schedule. I aim to have them finished well before the summer ends. Ionna has her book deadline. I have my building contracts deadlines. My work will be achievable in the warm, drier weather.' Previously, he'd been scuppered by the early winter snow and lashing rain. Leith sounded determined, but hid his true feelings about Ionna's arrival. There were things to consider, forged in the fire of hard choices.

Effy phoned Donal. 'I've told Ionna you're on your way, and to stay in the car as you suggested.'

'I'll be there soon with the tractor.' Donal didn't add that Leith would be with him.

Leith overheard the conversation.

'She says she took the forest route, against my warning about the mud, because she thought I was just saying that to keep her from running into the laird,' Effy explained.

'Roary is busy working in the castle,' Donal assured her. 'He's none the wiser about the mire she's in. I aim to keep it that way.'

'I appreciate your help,' said Effy.

The call ended and Donal put his phone in his pocket as they approached the tractor he aimed to use for the rescue. It was outside a barn. He threw a couple of large mats to use as traction boards into the back, a shovel, checked he had a chain and heavy duty strap, and then climbed in and started it up. Years of experience using a tractor for all sorts of tricky situations ensured he knew what to take with him. The car didn't need towed, it just had to be unstuck.

Leith got in the passenger seat.

Donal drove over the farmland to the forest where the old route wound its way down.

And there was Ionna's shiny new red car stuck in the mud ahead of them in the forest road that was barely used these days. Another road down between the fields was the main thoroughfare now.

'She's not too deep in the mud,' Donal assessed. 'A wee pull and we'll have her on the road again.'

Overarching trees shaded the fading sunlight, preventing Leith from seeing clearly the petite figure sitting in the driver's seat.

Before she'd even noticed them, Donal turned the tractor around and started to reverse towards the front of her car. 'I'll attach the chain and the strap.'

'How can I help?'

'Shove the mats under the front tyres...' Donal's words faded as Leith's memories rushed over him in a torrent of emotions.

Leith's heart pounded. The last time he'd seen her was when she drove away from Effy's cottage six years ago. He'd argued with her that morning. But seeing her leaving, he'd run from his cottage to try and...what? Stop her? Tell her he loved her more than anything?

Inwardly, he relived those last moments, still trying to think if he could've done something different to change her mind. Feeling like a part of his soul was being ripped away from him, he hadn't said a word. He just stood beside her car gazing down at her through the open window, breathless from the speed he'd run from his cottage.

Ionna had looked at him as if she'd never see him again. Those violet–blue eyes could etch through a man's heart like nothing he'd ever felt since the day she left. The beautiful heartbreaker had left her mark on him. The laird was right. He still had the battle scars. The fight to win her heart was lost because he knew, everyone knew, it was Roary she loved.

'...Use the shovel if you have to scoop away some of the muck.' Donal's words of advice filtered back through to him.

Leith nodded, and they both jumped down from the tractor.

Donal began to unravel the chain and the straps. Leith grabbed the mats and the shovel. They walked towards the car, Donal leading the way, his tall, strapping build shielding Ionna from having a clear view of the man behind him.

Ionna perked up, seeing Donal, recognising the familiar friendly face, perhaps a bit more grizzled around the beard than before, but not by much. Her mind dismissed the second man, a farmhand she presumed, and sat up, relieved that Donal had arrived. She rolled the window down to talk to him.

But Donal bent down to check where the car's tow hook was and started to attach the chain and strap.

The second man was now standing beside her car on the driver's side. Her close–up view showed a lean–hipped man wearing jeans and a white T–shirt. He was so close to the car that she couldn't see his face. It was only when he leaned down and his pale blue eyes looked at her through the open window that she felt her world tilt at a giddying angle.

'Leith?' Ionna gasped, saying his name as if she questioned it was really him. She knew it was and yet, he was more handsome than ever. And he'd been handsome before, but she'd never seen him in the true light he deserved because he always stood in Roary's shadow. The one she'd created from her crush on the laird.

Leith's heart took a huge hit. There she was, looking at him again through the open window of her car. Time had gone full circle, adding a twist of fate. The violet–blue eyes were still gorgeous. Her long, silky blonde hair hung around the shoulders of her floral dress, and her porcelain skin added to her beautiful face. Every muscle in his stomach tensed from the effort to appear calm. Secretly, a storm of emotions was turning him inside out.

'Ionna.' His rich voice acknowledged her.

Then he bent down and jammed one of the mats under a tyre. She saw the ruffled head of auburn hair and the broad shoulders. Her mind calculated what he was doing there, and came up with the reason that he'd come along to help Donal.

She watched Leith walk around to the other side of the car and add a mat there too, after using a shovel to dig away some of the sludge that the tyre was wedged in.

Leith walked away and threw the shovel in the back of the tractor. She noted the strong, lean build, remembering how fit he used to be, forgetting just how tall he was. A match for the laird.

'I need you to switch the engine on,' Donal said to her. He was now standing at the driver's window. 'Put the car in first gear, then gently give it some revs and drive forward at my signal.'

With her senses in a whir, Ionna immediately turned on the ignition and thrust the car into first gear, keeping the handbrake on.

'No! Not yet,' Donal yelled.

In her panic to undo this, she accidentally pressed the accelerator, causing the tyres to spin in the mud and throw a wash of sludge at Leith as he walked towards the car. He jumped back, but it splashed a thick coating of mud over the front of his T–shirt.

Ionna stared at Leith through the windscreen, realising what she'd done.

'Calm down, Ionna,' Donal told her. There was nothing he could do about the mess Leith was in. He just needed to get the car unstuck. 'Try again. Nice and slow. On my signal.'

Ionna hesitated and looked flustered. She wished she hadn't taken the forest road. She'd been determined to arrive on time, and not cause any ructions. Now here she was in the midst of this drama involving Donal — and Leith, the last man she expected to see.

Donal waved Leith to come over.

'I have to drive the tractor,' Donal whispered to him. 'She's in no state to handle the car sensibly.'

Leith nodded, and Donal headed back to the tractor.

Taking a deep breath, Leith trailed his muddy T–shirt off and threw it aside.

Ionna tried not to stare at his fit physique. All smooth muscles rippling with raw masculinity.

Leith pulled the driver's side door open. 'Slide over.'

She'd made a mess of things, including him, but they had to get the car moving.

Ionna scrambled across to the passenger seat as the half–naked familiar stranger took charge behind the wheel.

The broad shoulders, strong arms and the sheer height of him made the car feel suddenly smaller. His fresh masculine scent reminded her of the sea, mixed with the forest's fragrant greenery.

Her heart reacted to his closeness, and she scolded herself for blushing. But most women would react to having a handsome man like Leith sitting next to them. Wouldn't they? Calm down, she told herself. Easier said than done.

Donal signalled to Leith and then they worked in tandem. The tractor's power pulled the car smoothly from the mud as Leith steered it carefully, using the lower gears to keep it steady.

Clear of the mud, Ionna still felt locked in the predicament. Maybe it was the excitement, the upset, whatever, but the adrenalin running through her didn't bode well for her handling the car safely to drive it to Effy's cottage.

'Are you okay?' Leith's voice cut through the atmosphere around them.

She blinked. 'I'm not...I need a few moments to...' Her hands were shaking, her senses in a whirl.

'I'll drive you home,' Leith offered.

Home? The word resonated in her heart. She was home again. And yet she wasn't. Everything was temporary. Just like her life in Edinburgh. Six years, and she'd never really settled down. Now here she was back in the village causing trouble like everyone would expect from her.

Donal jumped down from the tractor, unhooked the chain and strap from her car, and came over to talk to Leith. He leaned down and spoke through the open window. 'Everything okay?'

Leith's eyes signalled that it wasn't. 'I'm driving the car to Effy's cottage.'

Donal got the message. 'I'll take the tractor back. Thanks for stepping in to help.' He looked at Ionna. She was as lovely as ever, even more beautiful, but there was a sadness in her eyes. Maybe it was just tiredness from the long drive. 'Welcome home, lass,' he said gently.

'Thank you, Donal.' His kindness made her well up. But as he picked up the two mats and the muddy T–shirt, and walked away to the tractor, she stemmed the tears, not wanting to create any further drama, especially with Leith in such close proximity.

'Put your seatbelt on.' Leith pulled his across his smooth chest and secured it.

Her hand accidentally brushed against his as she clipped her belt in. The spark she felt made her jolt. Those blue eyes of his told her he'd felt it too. He noticed she wasn't wearing an engagement or wedding ring. And then he looked straight ahead, concentrating on driving the car out of the forest into the grassy clearing.

Within moments, the sea came into view. Ionna perked up, eager to see it after all these years. It looked the same. The picturesque turquoise seascape with white sand, hazy distant islands and cottages dotted along the upper part of the shore.

'It hasn't changed,' she said breathlessly, forgetting that Leith probably didn't want to chat to her or exchange pleasantries after their harsh goodbye so long ago. But the words were out before she could stop herself.

She had changed, Leith thought. Like Donal's impression, she was a true beauty, prettily dressed, and yet far more fragile than he'd expected. As if life had worn her down. Ionna had always been slender, and barely came up to his shoulders. But she'd never seemed to have a fragility to her, not as he remembered.

He'd seen the publicity photo of her on the back cover of her first embroidery book. Her next two books had the same photo. He imagined it was to coordinate her image. It was a lovely pose, but the only one available. Even used on her website. She didn't post on social media, so he'd no way of knowing what she looked like since she'd left, apart from that one picture.

She'd seen nothing of him. Leith wasn't online, and his building work hadn't been highlighted like the features about the laird and his castle. But she hadn't seen those either. The only people from her past that she'd seen updated photos of were Effy, from the picture on her craft website, and a couple of the other ladies from the local crafting bee. The ladies sold their quilts, knitting, crochet, embroidery and other crafts from their websites.

It felt like she'd stepped into the past, but hadn't properly accounted for the effects of time on the people she'd left behind. In her mind's eye she pictured they wouldn't have changed that much. She didn't think she had. The fragility that others noticed in her had crept up so slowly that she wasn't aware of it. Perhaps she'd noticed the tiredness in her eyes from the upset of her recent split with her boyfriend. And the pressure of the book deadline. But the fresh sea air and countryside would soon invigorate her.

'There's a water stand pipe over there,' said Leith. 'Do you want me to hose the mud off the car? It'll save Effy coming out with a bucket of water and sponge.'

'Yes, thanks.'

He parked the car. 'It'll only take a few minutes.'

Ionna stepped out of the car for fresh air while he hosed the mud away that was mainly on the tyres.

Seeing his brawny build, she tried not to stare, and not be affected by how handsome he was. She was overtired and overwrought she told herself and not inclined to let herself be affected.

While he was busy with the hose, she walked towards the sea to gaze out at it. She loved the forest, but the sea had always been her favourite. Swimming during the summer, or braving the colder days when the sea was brisk. Morning seaside walks to blow away the cobwebs of sleep and ignite her creativity to design new embroidery patterns. Afternoon tea by the sea, poured from a flask into a vintage china cup, served with a slice of Victoria sponge cake from a picnic basket, while sitting on a blanket, during the long amber autumns when the summer refused to give way to the new season. Winter walks along the shore when the sand was covered with snow. Nights, during any season, standing watching the sea shimmer under the vast starry sky. All those memories came flooding back...

'It's all done,' Leith called to her. Her car looked clean and new again.

Ionna wiped away the tears from her face, not realising she'd been crying.

Leith strode towards her. He didn't ask her if she was okay, because obviously she wasn't. He knew he wasn't in a position to comfort her, even though deep down, his instincts still made him want to put his arms around her and protect her from the harshness of the world.

But he did what he'd done in the past. He said nothing.

In Ionna's mind, no man she'd ever known could say so much with silence. And something in her clicked, released, and she felt more at ease with Leith. This was how it used to be between them. She'd cause trouble. He wouldn't scold her. That's why their last argument in the past had thrown her senses. They'd both said things they didn't mean. She knew she had. But the past was cast in stone and nothing could erase it.

'Would you like to get a breath of fresh sea air? Stretch your legs after the long drive?'

Ionna nodded, taking him up on his offer, and they fell into easy step with each other and walked down one of the pathways on to the white sand. From down there, level with the water, she could hear the sound of the sea gently lapping on to the shore.

Glancing up at the sky where the blue was battling to knock the greyness aside, she breathed deeply.

'It felt like summer this morning when I was up mending the roof of my cottage.' He glanced up on to the coastal area where his cottage stood along with the others. Raised by his grandfather, Leith had learned building work from him since he was a young boy. His grandfather passed when Leith was in his early twenties and he'd inherited the cottage.

'So you're still living there.' She'd sometimes wondered what had become of him. Imagining he'd be settled. He was the marrying type.

'Still there. I've established my building business. It's doing well.'

'I'm happy for you, Leith.'

He sensed no word of a lie, and gulped down a wave of emotion.

'I hear from Donal that you're working on a new embroidery book.'

'Yes, I've signed another three–book deal with my publishers.'

'Congratulations.'

She smiled her thanks. 'The deadline for the latest book is pretty tight, but I agreed to the deal, so...' She took another deep breath of sea air. 'Effy's letting me stay with her while I finish it. I'm here for the summer.'

'I've a deadline to finish two other cottages, as well as my own one. I invested some of my earnings into the other properties.'

'Planning to do them up and sell them on?'

'The deals are done. I just have to complete the renovations, refurbishments and decor.'

'The decor?'

'Yes, the deals include the cottages being walk–in ready. It's financially worthwhile, and I can decorate them even on rainy summer days.'

Ionna smiled. 'Effy says we're in for a scorcher of a summer.'

'Even better. I'll decorate with the windows open. And I'm tending to the gardens.'

'Mister all–round handyman builder.' She smiled as she crowned him with the title.

Leith smiled back at her, and for a flicker of a second, he forgot that they were on the clock and he had to drive her to Effy's cottage.

He stopped, and those broad shoulders of his blocked out the fading sunlight as she looked up at him.

'Donal will have phoned Effy to say we're on our way,' he said.

Ionna sighed heavily, and without either of them saying a word, they started to walk up from the shore and on to the coastal path that had a panoramic view of the sea.

'Is everyone else still living in the village?' she said as they headed back to the car.

'More or less. A few folk come and go. Some go away to the cities to university or training courses, but most of them come back. Others think they'll head away to experience living and working in a city or big town. Few stay away for long.' Except Ionna, but he buttoned his lips.

'I never really settled the way I imagined I would in Edinburgh,' she told him. 'But it was easy for travelling back and forth to my publishers. At first. It's less necessary now that we've established the format of the books and they've proved to be a success. Though I still have to travel to promote the books when they come out.'

'You've certainly made a success of your career,' he acknowledged.

She nodded. 'I love my embroidery work. But these past three books I've always been working so far ahead that I'm living out of season.'

He frowned.

'In summer I'll be designing Christmas holly and berries, snowmen, winter patterns. And then embroidering summer flowers, bees and butterflies in the heart of winter.' She sighed. 'It's made these past few years fly by. The six years feel more like three. It's hard for me to keep track of time as I become so steeped in whatever season I'm designing for.'

'What season is this new book?'

'No season. Just a mix of floral and nature patterns.' She gazed all around, from the sea to the green countryside and fields, and then the forest. 'There should be plenty of flowers, creatures and pretty cottages to create my designs from.'

They reached the car and he opened the passenger door for her.

'I might include the lovely flowers from your cottage garden in my designs.' It was the first time she'd smiled without underlying tension, and for a moment, he caught a glimpse of the mischievous look that he adored from her past.

Ionna got into the car, and watched the fine figure of Leith walk around and get in the driver's side.

'I'd offer you a top or a cardigan,' she said playfully, glancing at the craft boxes and luggage that was piled up in the back seat of her car. 'But I don't think they'd fit you.'

'Probably not my colour,' he said, joining in her playfulness.

'We could stop off at your cottage,' she suggested.

'We're already later than late. Effy's cottage is two minutes away.' He started up the car and drove off.

No argument from Ionna. She could become accustomed to having a gorgeous man, stripped to the waist, driving her around.

Leith hadn't planned on doing anything other than parking the car outside Effy's front garden and then walking back to his cottage.

But his plans went awry when Ionna slipped back into serious mode when she saw the cottage that had once been her home.

Instead of getting out of the car when he pulled up. She sat there looking deep in thought, clearly dwelling on things from the past.

Leith got out of the car. 'Do you want me to help carry your boxes and luggage to the front door?'

'Yes,' she said wistfully, stepping out and gazing at the flowers in the well–tended garden. The whitewashed cottage that she'd tried to convince Effy to paint sky blue. The pretty curtains on the windows were no doubt handmade, like most items such as quilts, cushions, table covers, tea cosies and other items for the kitchen. She remembered helping to pick the fabrics from Effy's stash and learning about mixing and matching prints and solid colours. Her paint box had been fabric, embroidery thread, crewel wool and yarn. The textures and effects you could create from sewing.

The living room was always tidy but a treasure trove of crafts. A dresser had shelves filled with a haberdashery of sewing and knitting. Old–fashioned sweetie jars and jam jars brimming with lace and velvet trims, beads, pearls and sparkling sequins.

Bundles of fabric were tidily stacked in a stash that had been carefully curated to include pre–cut quilting weight bundles, dress fabrics from cottons to silks and chiffon, and the lovely white cotton and linen that was used for most of the embroidery work. And threads galore.

Effy and the other ladies of the crafting bee made most of their own things, including dresses. Ionna wore a dress she'd made the previous year. Nothing fancy, just a traditional tea dress pattern and a floral print fabric. Embroidery was her first love, but other crafts, like dressmaking and quilting were included in her skills.

Inside the cottage, the embroidery bee had started. Effy was in the kitchen making tea, and the other ladies were helping to serve up the cakes and shortbread. Everything was home baked. The chatter circled around Ionna's impending arrival.

CHAPTER THREE

'Donal said Leith was driving and that they were on their way.' Effy set up the teapot and cups while the kettle boiled.

Effy's kitchen was as traditional as the other rooms in her bright and airy cottage. A sturdy wooden table and chairs had plates and cups set for the tea and cakes that were part of the regular bee nights. Several of the crafting bee ladies held quilting, embroidery, knitting and other craft evenings in their cottages, and they brought their home baking to contribute to the cosy nights of crafting and chatter.

Mairead put slices of raspberry jam and cream sponge on to a plate. 'They've probably stopped for a natter, to catch up on things, smooth over the raw edges of the past.'

'Unless Ionna has managed to get the two of them lost on the way,' Vaila joked.

'Leith was driving,' Effy reminded Vaila. 'Though maybe Ionna has got him into a pickle too.'

Vaila put pieces of shortbread on a plate. 'It must've been a shock for both of them seeing each other again.'

'Donal said they were quite civilised about their encounter,' Effy revealed.

'I wonder what Leith thought when he saw Ionna again,' said Jinnet, owner of the wee shop in the main street. Jinnet was in her forties with blonde hair, and enjoyed various crafts.

Ailish stirred milk into her cup of tea. A skilled quilter, she was attractive, thirty–one, and knew Ionna from school and living nearby. Her auburn hair was tied back in a ponytail, and flicked when she made it clear what she thought about Ionna returning to the village. 'I'm not going to lie, Effy. I think Ionna has a cheek waltzing back here and expecting you to sort out her muddle.'

'I can handle things,' Effy assured Ailish.

'And then there's the ruckus she'll cause with the laird,' Ailish added. 'Will she be throwing herself at him again like she did before she left? After all, he's the reason she ran away to Edinburgh.'

'There were other factors involved,' Effy told her. 'Including her book deal.'

'Yes, but what a furore she caused for Roary,' said Ailish.

'Ionna was the most beautiful young woman in the village, but it never brought her love and happiness,' Jinnet commented. 'And from what you said about her being dumped recently by her boyfriend in Edinburgh, it sounds like she's had no luck when it comes to romance.'

Effy tightened the straps on her apron and sighed.

'I'm not getting at you, Effy,' said Jinnet. 'I just don't like to see you being burdened for the summer. It's not fair on you, especially as you'd planned your holidays.'

'I'll have my trips around Scotland in the autumn,' said Effy, no umbrage taken.

'Ionna always had a big tip for herself,' said Ailish. 'She knew men fancied her. Just not the one she wanted. Poor Leith. His hopes got flattened like a pancake.'

Bhictoria chipped–in a remark. Bhictoria and her husband, Brochan, both in their fifties, owned and ran the local bar restaurant, referred to as the hub. 'Ionna was a wee bitty snooty at times. I won't be putting up with her nonsense.'

'Effy?' The familiar voice filtered through to the kitchen that adjoined the living room.

'Ionna's here!' Effy hissed, hoping she hadn't overheard them gossiping about her.

Cups rattled as the ladies jostled to hurry up and sort the tea.

Effy whipped her apron off and stepped into the living room ready to welcome Ionna, but was taken aback when she saw Leith, stripped to the waist, carrying one of the large packing boxes filled with Ionna's embroidery work.

'Where do you want me to put this?' Leith said to Effy.

'Eh, through there in the spare bedroom.' Effy gestured to the room across the hallway and tried not to look flummoxed.

Leaving Ionna standing in the living room, Leith carried the box through.

Effy had planned to welcome Ionna properly, expecting she'd open the cottage door and invite her in. But seeing her niece standing there in the living room looking...lost, almost fragile, as if life had knocked some of the stuffing out of her, she faltered for a moment and then smiled.

'Welcome home, Ionna.' Effy moved close and gave her a hug.

'It's great to see you, Effy.' Ionna smiled and tried not to well up again. She had a shopping bag and handbag with her and put them down on one of the chairs that were set up for the bee night.

The other ladies peered through from the kitchen, whispering, as Leith headed back out to bring in more boxes. They saw a glimpse of him as he used the hallway rather than parade himself through the living room again.

'That was fast work,' Ailish whispered. 'She's got the shirt off Leith's back before she's even had a cup of tea.'

Jinnet pursed her lips in disapproval at Ionna. 'What a wee minx.'

'I'll give you a hand,' Ionna called to Leith.

'No need,' he said, striding outside. 'I'll have everything unpacked in a jiffy.'

The whispering from the ladies in the kitchen continued. But from sniping about her, they began to sound less inclined to criticise as they studied her while she chatted to Effy.

'Ionna still looks beautiful, but she seems tired...'

'A lovely shadow of her former self...'

'Probably all the upset of the split from her ex–boyfriend...'

'He didnae sound nice...'

'Nooo...'

'Heartbroken...'

'World weary...'

'She's come to the right place to heal...'

'Get her strength back...'

'Fresh sea air and guid home cooking...'

'We should go through and say hello...'

The ladies stepped from the kitchen into the living room to welcome Ionna.

'It's nice to see you again,' said Mairead.

'And you, Mairead.'

Leith, laden with craft boxes stuffed with embroidery thread, hoops and patterns, walked past in the hallway, but the ladies didn't falter in their welcome to Ionna.

'You've changed your hair,' Ionna said to Jinnet.

Jinnet touched her recently blonded locks. 'I thought I'd go a few shades lighter for the summer.'

'It suits you.' Ionna's comment was genuine.

'Are you still doing your knitwear modelling?' Ionna thought Vaila looked lovelier than ever and had done well with her model work before.

'I am,' Vaila confirmed, surprised Ionna even remembered or was willing to acknowledge it. Vaila, like a few other women in the village, had a fancy for the laird. Though none of them had made a blatant play for him like Ionna had.

'Is the hub still buzzing these days?' Ionna said to Bhictoria.

'It is. We've extended the function room at the back of the bar to make the floor bigger for the ceilidh dancing nights,' Bhictoria told her.

Ionna had a faraway look. 'I can't remember the last time I went to a ceilidh. It's been years.'

'Did you not go to ceilidhs in Edinburgh?' said Bhictoria.

'No, I...became too busy, wrapped up in my work.' The closest to the truth she could reveal. Her ex–boyfriend wasn't keen on ceilidhs. And the first two years in Edinburgh had been hectic, unsettled.

Bhictoria brightened. 'There's a ceilidh night at the hub soon. Come along. And we've got a new menu for the summer. Drop by for lunch or dinner once you're settled in.'

'I will,' said Ionna. 'I'll buy a pair of suitable shoes for dancing in, and rummage through my clothes for a dress.'

'The nice dress you're wearing and the flat pumps will do just fine,' Bhictoria assured her.

'I've dresses you can wear,' said Effy, igniting offers from the other ladies to kit her out too.

'I tend to live in jeans and tops these days,' Ionna told them. 'Though I made this dress myself.' And wore it to present the right impression, even though her three pairs of jeans outweighed the rest of the items in her clothes luggage.

'You used to love buying vintage clothes and mending them to wear, creating your own style,' said Effy.

'I intend getting back to buying pre–loved clothes,' Ionna said, revealing more of her plans. 'Rewinding to fashions I used to love wearing. Sewing and mending them with embroidery.'

Effy's sewing machine sat on a table in a corner of the living room. Fabric was folded beside it. A quilt she'd been making. Though she could run up a classic wrap or tea dress easily using patterns from the folders tucked on a shelf. 'I'll run up wee dresses for you too.'

Other offers came in from all angles as the women realised that Ionna needed bolstered during her stay.

'Right,' said Effy. 'I'm sure you're gasping for a cup of tea. We've just made a fresh pot and there's home baking if you're peckish.'

Ionna had skipped breakfast, wanting to be on her way from Edinburgh, and planned to make pit stops en route, that didn't pan out when she took two wrong routes on the map. Lunch had been a bite of a sandwich and a few slurps of tea. She picked up the shopping bag. 'I wasn't sure what to bring for the embroidery bee night.' She offered up a packet of chocolate digestive biscuits purchased from a service station.

Effy bit her lip and almost felt like crying for her. The other women fell silent, seeing the effort Ionna had made not to turn up to a bee night empty–handed.

Mairead came through with a plate of the delicious jam and cream cake slices in one hand and Effy's melt in the mouth shortbread petticoat tails in the other.

Ailish followed behind Mairead carrying slices of rich fruit cake decorated with glacé cherries, and cupcakes topped with buttercream.

Effy accepted the chocolate biscuits as if they were ideal. 'I fair enjoy a choccie biccie with my tea.' She took the biscuits through to the kitchen.

Leith finished unloading the inside of the car, and went round to the back and opened the boot. Expecting to see it brim full with luggage, he was taken aback by the three suitcases. Was that it? The sum total of Ionna's belongings? The boxes were see–through and were clearly filled with her embroidery and craft work.

He'd noticed a cardboard box in one of them labelled a light box, and it was in with her laptop and artist materials, mainly sketch pads, pens and pencils. Where were the things she'd accumulated during these past years? Three suitcases of clothes. Was that it?

Picking up all three suitcases, he closed the boot and carried them inside.

'Leith took it off so he didn't muddy my car,' Ionna finished explaining to the ladies.

He pretended not to overhear, and put the cases down in the bedroom, beside the bed that looked so comfy with its lovely quilt. Effy had made everything look welcoming, from the bedside lamp that would give a cosy glow in the evenings, to the pretty curtains hanging on the window that offered a view of the back garden and the forest beyond.

Taking a final look, as he doubted he'd see Ionna's bedroom again, he went through to the hall and stepped briefly into the living room.

'That's everything brought in from your car, Ionna. Are you having the rest of your belongings delivered later?'

'No, that's everything,' said Ionna. 'I rented accommodation in Edinburgh so I don't have much stuff.'

It was on the tip of his tongue to tell her he didn't expect to find furniture in her belongings, but surely there was more than this. He pressed his lips firmly together.

Ionna stood up. 'I'll walk you out.'

The ladies sensed the tension.

'Would you like a cup of tea before you go?' Effy said to Leith.

'No, I'll be on my way.' Then he saw the plate of shortbread. 'I'll grab a piece of your shortbread though, Effy.' He picked up a piece and took it with him as Ionna walked him out.

Digging into the pocket of his jeans, he handed her the car keys.

She almost gave him a hug to thank him for helping her, then stepped back. Instead, she stood upright, nowhere near his shoulder height, but standing as confident as she could. 'I appreciate you helping me.'

'Enjoy your summer, Ionna. And all the best with your new book.'

The blue eyes gazed down at her, breaking her heart a little. He knew her well, or at least better than other men. Leith, she believed, saw her for what she was, had always been. Far from perfect. A magnet for trouble. With a past crush on the wrong man.

He didn't say anything else. Then he smiled gently and walked away towards his cottage further along the shore.

The sea air blew through her blonde hair, and she swept it back from her face as she watched his tall, lean figure for a few moments before turning around and going back into Effy's cottage.

She overheard the ladies talking about her as she went in and hesitated in the hallway.

'How in the name of the wee man did she not fancy Leith?' Jinnet exclaimed. 'He's gorgeous.'

'She had too strong a crush on the laird,' said Effy.

'I sensed a spark between her and Leith today,' Mairead confided.

A couple of others agreed.

Effy doused any hope of them getting together. 'Ionna isn't moving back to the village. And Leith won't move to live in Edinburgh. He's not a city type.'

'We could maybe see a summer fling?' Jinnet suggested.

'No,' said Effy. 'Ionna isn't looking for romance while she's here. She told me she wants to concentrate on finishing her book.'

Feeling awkward that she was overhearing things, Ionna rattled her car keys, put them down on the hall table and walked into the living room.

'These are some of the new colours of embroidery thread,' said Effy.

'The blue tones are perfect for summer embroidery patterns,' Mairead remarked.

'Ah, there you are, Ionna.' Effy stood up. 'I made a pot of broth. Would you like a bowl? I could heat it up while I make another round of tea.'

'Yes, thank you,' Ionna gladly accepted and followed Effy through to the kitchen while the ladies had their tea and cake. 'Let me give you a hand.'

The kitchen was familiar to Ionna and she filled the kettle for tea, remembering that the teabags were kept in the caddy on the shelf near the cooker, and what drawer the teaspoons were in.

Effy heated the broth and cut two thick slices of bread from a farmhouse loaf and put them on a plate.

'You can have your soup in the living room,' Effy offered.

'It's fine, I'll have it here in the kitchen and then come through to see the new embroidery thread.' Ionna rinsed the large ceramic teapot, and added the teabags as the kettle came to the boil.

Effy sensed the tension in the kitchen. 'If you overheard us gossiping about you, we're not being snippy. We're just concerned about you.'

'I know.' Ionna made the tea. 'It was a shock seeing Leith after all these years,' she admitted. 'And he is handsome, but I'm really not looking for romance. As for Roary...the crush I had on him faded fairly soon when I moved to Edinburgh.'

'I never liked to ask, and you didn't speak about him.'

'Moving away was the best thing for me. It showed that it was just a crush I had on Roary. Not a deep, lasting love. I became too busy finding a flat in the city, working with my publishers, having to travel to meetings with them. The hectic schedule left little room for romance. It's only in the last three years that I've seriously dated, and I seem to have a knack for picking men that disapprove of everything from my embroidery work to my love of vintage clothes.'

'You always loved wearing vintage. The bargains you used to find and then mend or embroider with your lovely motifs were wonderful. I was surprised when you said you didn't have much of a wardrobe to bring with you. You loved your vintage fashion.'

'I still do. But I discarded a lot of the clothes I'd accumulated. My ex used to wonder why I liked to wear old stuff, as he called it, when I could afford something new. Before I left Edinburgh, I gave away

41

the dresses and outfits I wore when I was dating him. And the wrong choice before him. I wanted to leave the breakup memories behind. But I'm planning to splurge on vintage bargains again while I'm here.'

'I'm glad, because I found three of your old dresses that I'd kept tucked away. They were too lovely to throw out. And I suppose I hoped one day you'd come back and claim them. Even if it was just for a visit.'

'Which ones?'

'The classics. The white broderie anglaise dress. The pale blue chambray. And the cornflower blue cotton.'

Ionna's face lit up with a smile. 'Those were my favourites. The more they were washed, the lovelier they became. The fabrics softened beautifully.'

'I laundered them and hung them in your wardrobe.'

'I can't wait to see them again and try them on.'

'Eat your broth first.' Effy used a ladle to serve the soup. She added a dash of black pepper. 'There you are. I hope you enjoy it.'

Ionna sat down ready to tuck in.

'Come through and join us when you're finished.'

'I don't want to interrupt your bee night.'

'You're not. We'd love to hear about your new embroidery designs.' Effy picked up the pot of tea and carried it through to the living room.

Eating her soup and bread, Ionna listened to the chat filtering through from the ladies as they discussed their embroidery, quilting, knitting and other crafts.

Sitting in the cosy kitchen, it was the first time in a long while that she'd felt at home.

CHAPTER FOUR

After finishing her broth, Ionna joined the other ladies in the living room. A seat had been kept for her beside Effy. They were working on their embroidery, mainly stitching designs on white cotton fabric in hoops. One woman was knitting, attending the bee for the crafting and chatter.

'I'll bring my embroidery through.' Ionna went into the bedroom, dug out the embroidery she'd been sewing before she left Edinburgh, along with a craft box filled with thread.

Sitting down to rejoin the others, she showed them the floral pattern she was embroidering. 'It's a heart of forget–me–nots.'

'The colours of the wee blue flowers are lovely,' said Effy.

'It's one of the designs for the new book,' Ionna explained as her embroidery in the hoop was passed around for the others to see. 'A classic design. The pages in the book are roughly the same size as an A4 sheet of white paper. This will be on one page with a couple of small forget–me–not motifs. One of those will be a three–flower sprig, and the other a single flower. And there will be floral lettering.'

'They're one of my favourite flowers,' said Jinnet, admiring the satin stitched petals.

'Mine too,' Mairead added.

The hoop was passed around full circle and then given back to Ionna. She elaborated on the design. 'I used two strands of embroidery floss to satin stitch the petals, the centres and the leaves. The heart shape is back stitch.'

'What type of patterns are you having in your new book?' said Ailish. 'Your other books had seasonal themes.'

'The new book isn't seasonal,' Ionna explained. 'The patterns will be lots of floral and nature designs.'

'How do you create the patterns for the books?' said Effy. 'You used to draw your own designs by hand.'

Ionna picked up her sketch pad. 'These are my sketches. I've inked quite a few of the pencil drawings into finished artwork so that I can embroider the patterns and see if they work. The illustrations are sent off to the publishers so they can start to format the book. And I send the editorial, the instructions for each pattern — the colours and types of thread and the stitches and methods.'

'It's a lot of work,' Effy remarked.

'It is,' Ionna agreed. 'But I've finished some of it and I just need to keep creating new designs.'

Effy flicked carefully through the sketchbook. 'You were always a talented artist. I can recognise all these flowers from your sketches — roses, pansies, bluebells and cornflowers.'

'They're artistic versions of real flowers,' Ionna explained. 'And so are the bees, butterflies, ladybirds, dragonflies and other wee creatures.'

'I wish I could draw,' said Vaila. 'I'll certainly buy your new book when it comes out to embroider these patterns.'

Effy reached up and took Ionna's previously published books down from a shelf. 'These are beautiful books. If the new one is anything like them, you'll have another success. There are so many lovely patterns in each book.'

'I'm looking forward to working on the remainder of my designs here,' said Ionna. 'You'll see me wandering around gazing at the flowers and the scenery with a pencil and paper.'

'You have lots of pretty scenery and flowers to select from,' said Effy.

'I noticed the flowers in your front garden,' Ionna said to Effy. 'I'll sketch some of those. I'm putting my favourite flowers in the new book, variations of everything from cornflowers to sunflowers. And thistles. I want to include a crewel wool thistle and use a soft lilac colour to create a wispy effect on the top.'

'I ordered crewel wool along with the new embroidery thread.' Effy handed Ionna a small craft box. 'There are pale lilac and purple tones.'

Ionna felt the softness of the crewel wool and lifted up the small skeins, mixing and matching the colours. 'These would be perfect for a thistle embroidery.'

'Take what you need to try out your designs,' said Effy.

'I don't want to take all your new colours, Effy.'

'Ach, I'm always ordering thread for my embroidery. Help yourself.'

Ionna picked four small skeins of the crewel wool.

'In the fields nearby there are thistles that you could sketch,' Effy suggested.

'Wonderful,' Ionna exclaimed. 'I love drawing from real life, though obviously I refer to photos as well. I take a lot of my own pictures and then work from them.'

'Pop into my garden,' said Ailish. 'I'm still living in my parents' cottage. They're away this year to the city due to my dad's work. The garden is blooming with flowers.'

'Thanks, Ailish. I will.'

'And I'm having a quilting bee evening tomorrow night,' Ailish added. 'Come along. Bring your embroidery if you'd prefer that to quilting.'

The evening continued with Ionna joining in the chatter and exchanging ideas for their embroidery.

Effy sold items she embroidered including cushions and pillows, along with embroidery in hoops and frames that customers put up on their walls as decorative pieces of art. She made kits comprising the pattern transferred on to a piece of white cotton or linen fabric, a hoop, needles and thread. These handy kits were popular and she sold these and her other products on her website. Additionally, she sold the quilts she made.

Although most of the ladies had websites and sold their crafts, running their small but successful businesses, others crafted only for themselves.

Jinnet was often to be found embroidering or knitting while she was tending to her wee shop in the main street. Her cottage was near the back of the shop.

Bhictoria had brought the table cover she was embroidering around the edges with flowers, but planned to use it in her cottage rather than sell it.

Ionna was still catching up on all the local news and gossip as the embroidery bee evening came to a close. The ladies started to pack up their craft bags.

'We'll tell you more gossip tomorrow night at my quilting bee,' Ailish said to Ionna, carefully tucking away her hoop embroidery.

'There's always plenty of gossip in this wee village,' said Effy.

Ionna knew she would be one of the latest topics, but she'd enjoyed finding out about the changes in the village since she'd left.

As Effy put Ionna's books back up on the shelf, the copy of the magazine with Roary on the front cover fell down.

Ionna picked it up from the carpet and recognised the laird's face. Roary had matured, but time had made him more handsome. His intense green eyes peered out from the photo. He wore a vintage tailcoat with a white shirt and cravat, looking like he belonged to a bygone era. He was certainly part of Ionna's past, but these stylish clothes created a look that fitted with him being the laird of a castle.

The cheery chatter stopped as Effy and the ladies wondered what Ionna's reaction would be.

Nothing. Even Ionna was surprised by this. Her heart didn't jolt. She didn't feel a pang of longing for the laird. Not at all. Not these days. Just an empty sense of resignation that this part of her past was over. It had been over for a long time.

Ionna flicked through the magazine to find the feature on the laird. There were several other pictures showing him standing outside the castle wearing his

48

traditional kilt, in the large function room surrounded by its historic architecture and paintings, descending the tartan carpeted staircase. And sitting in his living room wearing black trousers and an open neck white ghillie shirt with the laces undone, beside the roaring log fire. A chess board was set up on the table next to him.

'He's not smiling in any of the pictures,' Ionna remarked. There was a sense of magnificence mixed with melancholy to the images.

'The laird rations his smiles. You should know that,' Effy reminded her.

Ionna did remember. Somehow, it had given him an air of drama that had appealed to her younger self, but didn't impress her now. 'I barely remember Roary ever laughing, not heartily. He looks like a very serious man.'

The silence from the women showed they agreed with her.

'Donal said the feature was written by a photo–journalist from the city,' said Effy. 'He wanted to write about the laird's determination to keep his castle private and not open it up for tours or make it into a hotel.'

'The years have honed his handsomeness,' Ionna assessed. 'But I'm looking at a man with the weight of the world on his broad shoulders and in need of a smile.' She closed the magazine and put it up on the shelf, intending to read the feature later. Right now, a trip down that shadowy memory lane was taking the gid aff the cheery bee night.

Ionna brightened, wanting it to end on a happy note. 'Thanks for making me feel welcome again,' she said to the ladies. 'And I'll pop along to the quilting bee tomorrow evening to catch up on more gossip.'

Ailish shrugged her craft bag up on to her shoulder and smiled. 'There's always plenty of gossip. Nothing stays hidden around here for long.'

Effy and Ionna walked the ladies out and waved them off.

Ionna breathed in the fresh evening air before Effy closed the front door.

Effy picked up some of the cups on her way to the kitchen. 'I'll make you a cup of tea to settle you and then I'm sure you'll want to get to your bed.'

Ionna helped to clear the rest of the cups and plates and joined Effy in the kitchen. 'I'm all at sixes and sevens. I don't know that I can just fall asleep. My mind's buzzing with everything that has happened since I arrived.'

'Starting with getting stuck in the mud,' Effy said with laughter in her voice.

Ionna washed and dried the dishes while Effy made the tea. 'That'll be old gossip by the morning.'

'Aye, but the night's not over yet. Away through and read the magazine feature while I make us a cuppa.'

'And I used the tractor to pull her car out of the mud,' Donal told Roary.

The laird sat in the traditional living room beside the unlit fire. A half finished game of chess was on the board. Roary often liked to relax in the evenings on his own, reading a book from his library, or replaying the chess games of grandmasters from yesteryear.

The gossip had eventually filtered through to the laird, overhearing the castle's staff talking about Ionna's troublesome arrival. He'd called Donal in to hear what had happened.

Donal told him the details. 'Leith helped me,' he finally revealed.

'Leith? That was a fast move. Is he still hoping to win her heart? She'll only break his again.'

'I don't know his intentions regarding Ionna. I think he just wanted to give me a hand. But I will say that she's more beautiful than ever.'

'It's of no consequence to me.' Roary heard the brusqueness in his tone, and then relented. 'Thank you for handling the situation tactfully, Donal.'

'I'll leave you to get on with your game, Roary.'

'Still not inclined to play chess?'

'Dominoes down at the hub is more my taste. See you in the morning.' Donal started to walk away and then stopped. 'Gorden has left a supper for you in the kitchen. He says you didnae eat your dinner.'

The laird acknowledged the message from the castle's chef, and then watched Donal walk out of the living room. Several staff helped with the running of the castle and some of them, like Donal and Gorden, lived in cottages within the estate.

Roary lifted the black knight chess piece and made the next move. 'Check,' he murmured to himself, and then played on.

Effy and Ionna sat in the living room having their tea and talking about the feature.

Ionna skimmed over the summary of Roary's past. She knew he'd lost his mother when he was a wee boy and was raised as an only child by his father, the former laird. When his father passed, Roary was thrown into the role when only in his early twenties. Rather than balk at the burden of responsibility, Roary was up for the challenge and made a fine young laird.

It was the recent news that Ionna was interested in reading. 'It says that Roary takes his role as laird seriously, and travels regularly to London and other cities to secure business deals and investments that keep the castle solvent.'

'He does. He's not long back from a recent trip,' Effy confirmed.

'The feature quotes him as saying that the estate pays its own way, and the income from his investments helps with the upkeep of the castle.'

Wording under one of the pictures stated: *There is no lacklustre castle in Roary's world. Historic luxury, wealth and fortitude abounds.*

'The castle is well–maintained,' said Effy.

Ionna read another quote from the laird. '*The castle has always been my home, and I'm determined to keep it private and not turn it into a hotel.*'

'There are rumours that Roary would like to get married and have the castle as his family home,' Effy revealed.

'Is there anyone local that he's interested in?'

'No, and it's not for the lack of a few lassies trying, especially recently at the festive balls in the castle during the Christmas and New Year celebrations. Vaila is a wee bitty sweet on him, but he's not shown any interest in her, or Ailish or any local lassies. But they're not smitten the way you were, if you don't mind me saying. Vaila and Ailish have dated lads from the crofts, but it's no more than light flirtations and dancing at the hub when the party nights are on.'

'Where will Roary find someone to marry?'

'He's had girlfriends on his travels to the cities. Nothing serious. He's never brought any of them back to the castle,' said Effy. 'But there are always new lassies coming and going to the village, including women from the nearby town.'

'I'm sure Roary will find someone one day.'

'Aye. There comes a time when men like him have a longing to settle down.'

Ionna closed the magazine. 'I think I'll get ready for my bed now.' She finished her tea.

Effy put their cups in the kitchen while Ionna went through to her bedroom and flicked the bedside lamp on.

'If you're cold, I've folded another quilt.' Effy came through and opened the wardrobe door. 'It's on the top shelf here.'

Ionna's attention was drawn to the dresses that were hanging up. 'Are those the dresses you were talking about?'

Effy lifted the white broderie anglaise dress out of the wardrobe and held it up. 'Yes, they were too lovely to throw away.'

Ionna felt the texture of the fabric, remembering how it always made her feel fashionably chic when she wore it.

'Thank you for keeping them.'

Effy hung the dress back up and closed the wardrobe doors. 'I'll help you unpack in the morning. Not that you have a lot of clothes.'

'What I lack in clothes I make up for in crafts. But I intend to scour online for vintage buys that I can wear throughout the summer. Things I can sew and mend and decorate with embroidery, and take back with me to Edinburgh.'

'Well, you've all summer to splurge on pre–loved clothes, like you used to do. You were great at finding bargain buys and adding beautiful embroidery motifs.'

Ionna brightened. 'It'll give me ideas for new patterns.'

'Okay, I'll let you get some sleep.'

Leaving Ionna to get settled, Effy went through to her room and went to bed.

Tucked under the fresh sheets and the quilt, Ionna turned the bedside lamp off and gazed out the window at the view of the back garden, fields beyond, a sliver of trees from the edge of the forest, and a night sky so clear that she could see thousands of stars.

'Checkmate,' Roary muttered, easing off the tension from his shoulders and tidying up the chess board, setting it up for another game another time.

He wandered through to the kitchen in the silence of the castle that most nights, unless there was a function on, he had all to himself.

A light shone in the kitchen providing enough of a glow for him to see that Gorden had left him a hearty stew in a pot on the stove. Roary lit the cooker and while the stew heated, he helped himself to a slice of bread and butter and boiled the kettle for tea.

Pouring the stew into a bowl when it was ready, he sat at the kitchen table to eat his supper, rewinding the day, especially the news that Ionna was back and apparently more beautiful than ever. If this was true, and he'd no reason to doubt the gossip, a few local men's hearts were due to be broken during the summer. Not his, he reminded himself. Ionna was nothing but trouble, and that's the last thing he needed for a summer that promised to be a scorcher.

Leith lay in bed unable to sleep. He didn't need to ponder why. It was obvious. Ionna was back.

Maybe once the news sank in properly he'd feel more settled.

But his instincts warned him that the storm he'd sensed hadn't blown over. A feeling in his bones warned him that the whirlwind of trouble was going to pick up pace. He'd need all his strength to remain steady and work on his building contracts while being in the eye of the storm Ionna was brewing up.

Ionna couldn't sleep either, and that sense of mischief that often got her into a pickle was brewing.

In the past, when she was sure that Effy was sound asleep, she'd sneak out of the cottage and go for a walk, just down to the edge of the coast and gaze out at the shimmering sea.

55

Putting on her jeans, a top and a pair of training shoes, she opened the bedroom window and clambered out, smiling to herself, remembering that it was easy to step out of the window into the back garden. The front door used to click in the depths of the night and wake Effy, and she didn't want to risk doing that.

Standing in the garden, with a mischievous smile on her face, she checked that Effy's bedroom light hadn't switched on. Assured that she was free to go for a moonlit escapade for ten minutes, fifteen at the most, she picked her way across the garden, avoiding standing on the flowers, and stepped over the low fence. Glancing again at the darkened windows, she scurried round to the front of the cottage where she could view the sea nearby.

Hurrying along, glancing in all directions, checking that no one else was around, she ventured over to the grassy edge of the shoreline and gazed out at the mesmerising sea.

Waking with a jolt, Leith got out of bed and tried to shake the feeling of a storm crashing on to the shore. Worried that his senses were getting mixed up with thoughts of Ionna, he threw on his jeans, put on a pair of boots, and hurried outside to check that a real storm wasn't headed towards the coast. Local people warned each other of such events, ensuring that the community was safe.

Standing in his garden, he looked around and breathed in the atmosphere.

The vast sky looked clear of clouds and the air felt dry and calm, no hint of rain or far–off thunder rumbling across from the distant islands. Nothing. Except...was that Ionna standing there further along the shore? What was she doing at this late hour?

No rest for him this evening, Leith thought to himself, striding towards her. And no rest for troublemakers like Ionna even in the depths of the night.

CHAPTER FIVE

Walking down on to the sand, Ionna picked up a pebble and threw it into the glistening sea.

From behind her, another pebble came hurtling by, startling her as it fell into the deeper water beyond.

Jolting, Ionna looked round and then relaxed as she saw Leith walking towards her.

'Having fun?' His voice resonated in the sea air.

'Having trouble finding a shirt?'

'I was in bed.'

'Wearing jeans?'

'I don't wear anything in bed.' As soon as the words were out he regretted revealing this.

'Not even in winter? It gets pretty cold.'

Her smirk ignited another remark he would regret. 'I'm hot–blooded.'

'You've certainly got a blush on your cheeks.'

'I'm not blushing,' he lied.

'You're a bad liar.'

'I usually don't need to lie to anyone.'

'Then don't.' She picked up another pebble and rolled it around in her palm, giving him a challenging look. 'What are you doing here? An honest, half–naked, hot–blooded man like you?'

The frustration bubbled inside him. 'What are *you* doing here at this time of night?'

She threw the second pebble far out to sea, short of the distance Leith had thrown his, but close enough. 'Unwinding.'

'Wouldn't bed be the best place to unwind.' Another remark he wished he could undo, especially as Ionna was smirking at him again. 'What I mean is...after the long day you've had, that started at the crack of dawn in Edinburgh.'

'I'm used to working long and crazy hours, especially when I'm working on a book. Sometimes I'll sew way past midnight if I'm in a creative mood.'

The sound of his exasperated breath filtered out to sea. 'What are you really doing wandering around at this late hour?'

Her deep breath echoed his. 'Reliving a bit of the past. Some nights when I lived at Effy's cottage, I'd sneak out and come down here to the shore. No one else was ever around. I had the sea to myself when everyone was tucked up in bed. It always felt like an adventure.'

'There were times when your adventures got you into trouble.' His accusation bore the weight of truth.

'I don't deny it.' She turned to face the sea. 'I just wanted to feel that sense of excitement, outside in the depths of the night down the shore.' She gazed back at him. 'Be a little bit wild.'

Her words tore through his heart.

'But now I'm going to run back to the cottage. That's something else I haven't done in a long time — run, fast.' She used to love running. Not distance, even though she could. She preferred hundred metre sprints on the flat grassland along the coastal path, or on a quiet narrow road through the fields. The sand was too soft, the long grass too dense, the forest too gnarled. She liked to dash at speed.

Leith remembered. 'Running in the wild.'

Her smile lit up her face. 'You remember.'

'I do.' He pictured her lithe and limber figure running by the sea and the countryside. She wasn't out for a daily run like the laird. Her runs had a spontaneity and energy to them.

'You even joined me twice.' She bit her lip from reminding him she'd won by a country mile both times.

'Think you can still beat me?'

'Oh, I think that's a given.' She glanced at his boots. 'Tighten your laces, and let's go.'

Leith bent down and tied his laces.

'Remember the rules of running wild.'

Standing up, he rolled his shoulders, limbering up. 'What rules?'

'Exactly.' Her mischievous smile challenged him.

'Where do we start?'

'Right here. I'll race you full out to Effy's cottage. First to touch the front gate, wins.'

He was stronger than when she'd left the village. Faster for sure, though he didn't run for fun, sport, or any other reason. He ran when he needed to bring his tools inside out of the rain from a sudden downpour. Regular physical work had enhanced his strength and increased his hardiness. His lifestyle had built him up, whereas Ionna's chosen path had taken the edge off the vibrant and adventurous young woman he once knew. Could she still beat him in a race? Did he really want to dampen her daring attitude by winning?

'Don't hold back.' She sensed the reticence in him.

'I won't.'

Ionna led the way up from the sand on to the grassy coastal path where the ground was reasonably flat, hard and firm. Rather like Leith's chest and six–pack. Not that she was looking.

The whitewashed cottage was a short distance along from where they stood side by side as if in imaginary lanes ready to race.

'On the count of three,' she said.

Leith got into a sprinting stance, ready for an instant start. He believed he would win. He wouldn't hold back. She would know. But he wondered what her reaction would be.

'Don't be a grumpy loser,' she said.

'I admire your confidence.'

She got ready for the race. 'One...two...three!'

And they were off.

Ionna was fast off her mark and increased her pace, holding nothing back.

Leith was seconds behind her, watching her blonde hair whip in the wind she was creating from her pace. She was still fast. So was he, but not fast enough. This settled the outcome. It would be as it was before.

The distance was short but the race felt intense. He couldn't see the smile of joy on her face, feeling the sea air whip by her, running towards the cottage as she neared the agreed finishing line.

Her hand touched the gate first. A clear win. She had time to glance round and see Leith run full pelt towards the gate and skid to a stop. He placed both hands on the gate and leaned forward, kicking himself for being wangled into another showing up by the sprightly minx standing there with a triumphant grin on her face.

'You're faster than you were before,' she acknowledged.

'Not fast enough.' He wasn't out of breath, but he was all out of bravado. 'Congratulations, you win!' he announced loudly.

'Shh! You'll wake Effy.'

He glanced at the darkened windows of the pretty cottage wondering if a light would flick on. Nothing. He stepped back out of clear view anyway.

The smooth contours of his bare chest and arms were highlighted in the nightglow, and Ionna felt her heart react to him. Surely most women would, she told herself. Or maybe her heart was beating fast from the running. Dismissing this as an instant lie, she brought the night to a close.

'I've had a long day, starting with a crack of dawn drive from Edinburgh, and then sidelined by an impromptu rescue, which I'm still grateful for, an embroidery bee evening, and then challenged to a race by a hot–blooded, shirtless storm hunter. I really should get to bed to...unwind.'

Her mischievous smile melted his heart and split it in two. Let her go, one part of him warned. She didn't love you before. She won't love you now. Versus, invite her to have dinner with him sometime, anytime, tomorrow evening, and see if bridges could be mended and rebuilt without Roary being part of things.

'Goodnight, Leith. Enjoy your summer.'

She'd made his decision for him. He smiled tightly, turned around and walked away.

He heard bushes rustle as she clambered over the fence and disappeared round the back of the cottage to climb in her bedroom window.

A narrow escape he told himself firmly. He'd almost succumbed to being a fool again. Not this time, he chided himself. He wasn't changing his plans for the summer.

In the pale glow shining in her bedroom window, Ionna got ready for bed, snuggled under the sheets and pulled the quilt up, peering out at the view of the starry sky and countryside scenery.

Rewinding her encounter with Leith, night running with him, the sense of adventure, reminded her so much of the past that Roary's handsome face from the magazine photos filtered through. It disturbed her that she'd felt nothing for Roary seeing him again. Surely, there would be a pang of regret at what might have been? Was her heart protecting itself by pretending that she'd run out of feelings for him?

Fluffing her pillows, she settled down to get some sleep, deciding that adventures like sneaking out of the cottage at night could be relived. But she'd stopped loving Roary a long time ago. Those feelings couldn't be reignited, if her heart was telling her the truth.

She'd no future here in the village, she reminded herself firmly. In the morning, she'd concentrate on what she was here for. To finish her book.

Leith kicked his boots off and padded into his bedroom. He stripped off his jeans and got into bed. Don't dream about any storms, he told himself. Involving wind, waves, thunder and lightning, or the whirlwind of trouble tucked up in her bed in the cottage he could see in the distance from his window.

Get some sleep. There was building work to be done in the morning. Bricks and mortar type. Not emotional bridges he shouldn't risk crossing.

Wearing the pale blue chambray dress and a pair of gingham pumps, Ionna went through to the cottage kitchen the next morning.

Effy stirred a pot of porridge on the stove. 'Do you still like porridge for your breakfast?'

'Yes.'

Two bowls were set up on the table along with a pot of freshly brewed tea. Ionna poured two mugs of tea for them while Effy dished up the porridge, topping it with creamy milk.

They sat down to eat their breakfast, and Effy complimented Ionna on her blue dress. 'It's nice to see you wearing it. There's barely a cloud in the sky this morning, so I think we're in for a fine, sunny day.'

'I plan to make the most of it, and sketch those thistles you suggested.'

'Did you sleep well?' Effy wondered how she'd settled on her first night at the cottage.

'I slept great.' Then she confessed about sneaking out and her late night run with Leith.

All Effy did was laugh. 'You bring these situations on yourself.'

'It wasn't intentional.' Ionna continued to eat her porridge.

'Nonsense. You climbed out the window. You didn't inadvertently tumble out of it.'

64

'I just wanted a wee adventure.'

'I think you got it.' Effy cupped her mug of tea and looked at Ionna across the table. 'Did you win the race?'

'I did. And he wasn't wearing a shirt,' she added.

'There's a novelty.'

They giggled and finished their breakfast while they chatted.

'Leith has grown into a fine, handsome man,' said Effy.

'Romance isn't in my plans this summer.'

'You'd better make that clear to Leith.'

'I will, if I meet him again when he's half–dressed and hot–blooded.'

There was more giggling as Ionna relayed his comments.

'It sounds like he revealed more to you than his bare chest and muscles.'

'I think he wished he hadn't as he looked embarrassed.'

'No wonder.'

Ionna sipped her tea. 'But I'm going to be busy with my book, so I won't be teasing Leith, or any other man.'

'Like the laird?'

'Especially Roary. If he stays hidden in his castle, I probably won't even see him, unless he turns up to the ceilidh dancing at the hub. He never used to.'

'He still doesn't. I don't think he's seen the function room extension, and that was built months ago. Leith was the architect and the main builder.'

'Does Leith go to the ceilidhs?'

'Hardly ever. But maybe he'll look out his kilt and brogues now that you're here.'

Ionna topped up their tea. 'Do all the men wear kilts?'

'No, but Brochan does and he encourages the other men to get their kilts on for the ceilidh dancing. You'll be coming to the next ceilidh at the hub, won't you?'

'I will. I thought I'd wear the white broderie anglaise dress, if that would be appropriate.'

'Yes, perfect, and a pair of comfy shoes for dancing, like the ones you're wearing.'

Finishing their breakfast, Ionna helped to clear the dishes, then she packed her sketch pad and pencils and put them in an embroidered tote bag along with her phone.

Effy handed her a white cardigan she'd knitted. 'Put this on. It's a warm morning, but not scorching yet. And if you head into the forest, the trees shield the sunlight.'

'I'm not planning to go into the forest.'

'Best laid plans and all that...'

Ionna put the soft cardigan on, gave Effy a hug and headed out to find the thistles.

Leith woke up with a voracious appetite for a full–cooked breakfast. Checking the fridge for eggs, sliced Lorne sausage and other tasty ingredients, he knew a trip to the wee shop was in order.

After showering, he got dressed in jeans and a blue T–shirt, and walked to the shop.

The forest rising up the hillside shielded the little main street with its pretty shops and cobbled thoroughfare. While its back was protected from the elements, it faced the sea.

A canopy shaded the front window of Jinnet's shop from the direct sunlight. Vegetables and fruit were on display. Inside, the shelves were filled with various grocery products.

Freshly baked bread, rolls and scones were in an area near the counter. The fridges were stocked with milk, butter, cheese and other products along with cold drinks. A full shopping could be purchased from the wee shop, and Jinnet was happy to order in items that her customers requested. The shop doubled as the local post office and a courier service provided daily deliveries and pick ups.

Jinnet was serving another customer, so Leith started to pick up some of the groceries including milk, eggs, butter, tomatoes and a fresh loaf.

When the customer left, Jinnet started to ring up Leith's purchases, adding the slices of Lorne sausage and tattie scones he wanted as well.

'Having a hearty breakfast this morning?' said Jinnet.

'I'd a late night and woke up with an appetite. This should keep me going all day.'

'Working on the cottages?'

'Yes, I've sorted mine, except for the interior decor. The other two need exterior work. And one needs the extension finished.' He'd started work on the glass extension the previous week.

'This should keep you fired up.' Jinnet put the items in a bag and handed it to him as he paid for his groceries. 'Are you going to the ceilidh at the hub?'

'When is it on?'

'A couple of nights from now.'

'I might give my kilt an airing.' He hadn't gone to any of the local dance nights at the hub since the Hogmanay party at New Year.

'The ladies from the crafting bee will be joining in as usual, so Ionna will be there.'

The broad shoulders shrugged and he hid his reaction behind a casual smile. 'The more the merrier.'

'Yes, it should be a fun night.'

More customers came in as he left and headed back to his cottage. Over near the fields he saw Ionna. He would've waved if she'd seen him, but she was so far away and he assumed that she was getting on with the flower designs for her embroidery.

Cooking himself a hearty breakfast, he ate it sitting at his kitchen table while studying the plans for the extension on the cottage he aimed to work on that day.

He'd designed the large glass extension that would provide a panoramic view of the sea when it was finished. Glaziers from the nearby town had been hired to put the large windows and sliding glass doors in after he'd done the foundation work. Everything was going according to schedule and he aimed to keep it that way. No distractions, though he would maybe attend the ceilidh at the hub rather than sit at home and relax or go for an evening swim in the sea.

Night swimming was something he'd taken to during the past three years. He'd always gone for dooks during the day. The forest was on his doorstep, but he loved the sea with a passion. Rescuing Ionna and her car was the first time he'd been in the forest in a long while.

Pushing such thoughts aside, he studied the architectural plans and tucked into his breakfast.

His kitchen was functional rather than fashionable, and he'd installed a new cooker and other modern white goods. The remainder had an old–fashioned, homely look to it. And the wooden dresser and cupboards were as sturdy as the table and chairs.

Paint charts were clipped to one of the folders where he kept a note of all the building work and refurbishments for the cottages.

Fabric swatches and quilting weight fat quarter bundles sat on the dresser and were traditional floral prints and classic tone solids. Ailish had given him the samples and said she'd order the fabric when he'd decided what he needed. The crafting bee ladies were going to make new curtains and accessories for him. He'd pay for the materials and their skill and time.

The cottage with the extension would be the most luxurious, refurbished to a high level, walk–in ready, as agreed with the exclusive client that had bought the property. The sale had been a lucrative one for Leith. As was the other cottage he'd invested in, buying the two cottages and using his building skills and hard work to upgrade them.

Tins of paint were stored in a cupboard and he'd made a start on his cottage decor. The kitchen and living room were painted in shades of rich cream. Just the bathroom and two bedrooms to paint next. But first, he needed to knock a hole in the building work of the other cottages. Starting with tearing down part of a wall for the extension.

Tidying away his breakfast dishes, Leith got his tools ready, loaded up his van with other equipment, and drove the short distance along the coastal path to the cottage to start work.

Ionna sat on the grass and sketched the thistles, already picturing the designs she'd create. A lattice work thistle, a classic satin stitched one, and the crewelwork thistle with a wispy top like the ones that were blowing in the light breeze wafting up from the sea.

Snapping photos of the thistles with her phone, she noticed a blue haze at the edge of the forest through a gap in the thick trees. The bluebells! She remembered the bluebell wood in the forest. Scottish bluebells would be perfect for her book.

Packing up her artwork in her bag, she stood up, brushed the grass from her chambray dress, and headed towards the forest.

CHAPTER SIX

Scottish bluebells carpeted an area of the forest as Ionna stepped out of the bright sunlight into the shaded depths of the trees. Sunbeams flickered through the leaves on the branches, creating an effect like fairy lights or as if dragonflies were darting through the greenery.

In her upset at being stuck in her car, Ionna hadn't taken in the sheer beauty of the forest. Now here in the midst of the bluebells and clusters of pansies and other flowers, it was breathtaking. The fragrance was wonderful, like nature's aromatherapy.

Careful not to tread on any of the flowers, she followed a well–worn path through the bluebells, stopping in the depths of them. Sitting down on a tree stump, she shrugged her cardigan off, put it in her bag, and began sketching the bell–shaped flowers, emphasising the curve of the petals, picturing how she'd embroider these to create her patterns.

Happy that she had several drawings she could work from, she took photos of the flowers before moving on even deeper into the forest.

Seeing a hint of pink in the distance, she took another path, gnarled with tree roots that created natural steps leading up to an open patch where pink bluebells grew in all their pastel glory.

'Pink bluebells!' she murmured to herself. These would make a pretty addition to the book. As she sketched them, she started thinking what shades of pink embroidery thread she'd use to capture the colours. Offset with the gorgeous green stems and leaves, she imagined how nice these would be to stitch. Pink and green was such a lovely colour combination.

Roary ran through the forest on the last stretch of his morning run, dressed in his black training gear as always. A handsome shadow.

The laird welcomed the local community to wander in the forest, but he rarely came across many of them, especially in the mornings when the village was busy getting its day started. So when he saw the beautiful blonde young woman in the pale blue dress in the midst of the flowers, he skidded to a halt.

Ionna was so steeped in her artwork that she didn't notice the green eyes peering at her from across the swathes of bluebells. Hidden in the shadows of the trees, his dark clothing blending in, the camouflaged figure didn't disturb her.

Roary recognised Ionna, though the first impression that a fairylike waif was in the forest jarred his senses before he realised it was her. The troublemaker. The young woman he'd sidestepped years ago was home.

Should he alert her that he was there? Or run on without her even knowing? As he stepped back on to a broken branch, the sound resonated in the silence, alerting her that she had company.

She glanced round, at first not seeing the tall figure amid the trees, until the laird stepped forward. She recognised him in an instant. The dark flurry of hair, the broad shoulders narrowing down to his long, lean physique. There was no mistaking Roary. But had she made a mistake coming into the forest in search of flowers, and finding herself in trouble?

'Ionna.' His deep voice resonated through the forest, sounding as if it surrounded her as it disturbed the silence. The tone bore no reprimand of her being there. Not that she was doing anything wrong.

After waiting for a couple of seconds to hear if he had anything to say other than a single word, she replied in kind.

'Roary.'

The awkward acknowledgment of each other complete, he gave a curt nod and then ran off, disappearing into the trees, taking a well–used route of his back to the castle.

He didn't get far before he faltered, changed his mind and ran back.

Ionna shrugged off the very brief encounter and continued her artwork. She knew she was bound to come face–to–face with Roary during the summer. And she was in his territory, though the only reason she was there involved her search for flowers and foliage. He would assume otherwise.

She was mildly surprised that he even acknowledged her. Surely he could've run on and pretended he hadn't noticed.

And totally surprised when he reappeared out from the trees and ran over to her looking as handsome as the pictures in the magazine. Yet her heart didn't ache or react the way she thought it would seeing him again after all these years. Perhaps she'd grown up and was hardier than she realised, or she just didn't have any feelings for him now. The latter option rang true.

He wasn't smiling as he stopped in front of her.

Apart from his serious expression, she noted he wasn't out of breath. As fit as ever she surmised, gearing up to verbally defend herself regarding why she was there.

'Welcome back to the village, Ionna. I hear you're staying with Effy for the summer to work on your latest embroidery book.'

A welcome from Roary? And chit–chat? She was so taken aback that she hesitated.

He continued trying to make polite conversation while her mind whirled trying to fathom what was happening. Back in the day, she'd had such a crush on him that she'd often made a total fool of herself trying to gain his attention, his interest, his approval, and been rebuffed like someone flicking off a crumb. She still cringed, toe–curling cringes, when she rewound her flirty behaviour. The finale of her flirtations happened during the last ball at the castle. She'd invited him to dance with her and his refusal to even waltz socially with her at this celebration created such an uproar of reprimands from Effy and other women that she'd packed her bags that night and drove off the next day. After a huge quarrel with Leith to top off the trouble that had erupted.

Then she was gone for years.

Now she was back.

And Roary's handsome face was leaning down to admire her artwork. In what parallel universe had she stepped into?

'The bluebells you've sketched looked beautiful.' He gazed at her face. 'Really beautiful.'

Her heart reacted this time. Oh, yes. Thundering so hard she sensed he'd hear it.

Giving herself full marks for smiling, she replied casually. 'Thank you. The blue and pink bluebells are perfect for embroidery designs.'

'I've no knowledge of your techniques, but with your past success as an embroidery pattern designer, I'm sure you'll have lots of ideas.' He heard himself babbling, reasonably coherent.

He was still chatting to her? Suddenly suspicious, she glanced around wondering if he was keeping her talking until his cohorts came and turfed her off the estate. But there was no one else around. Just the two of them. So she relaxed and tried to be as sociable as him.

'Petals as pretty and delicate as these are ideal for satin stitching,' she said, keeping the conversation light. 'The blue tones are classic, and I think the pink will be gorgeous too. Different patterns on separate pages to make the most of the colours and designs.'

'Sounds excellent.' He hoped this was an appropriate phrase. His reaction to seeing her again had taken him aback. He'd behaved ungentlemanly in the past. The reasons were many, particularly his aversion to being involved in some dramatic romance when he wasn't yet settled into his role as the laird. And her reputation for being a troublemaker. All of this had shielded her true beauty from him. No wonder Leith had been smitten. And likely still was.

'Well, I'll let you get on with your art,' he said, sensing an awkwardness in the air, yet not knowing if it was coming from him or from her.

75

Ionna smiled pleasantly, and sat poised with her pencil ready to continue sketching a pink bluebell and a viola while she was there.

Roary ran off, chiding himself, and then double–backed. 'The rose garden is blooming profusely at the castle. You're welcome to come up and sketch there if it's of interest to you.'

It was. The rose garden was within the private part of the estate. The laird's exclusive garden. No one was permitted to wander there, ensuring that people wouldn't be able to peer in the castle's windows at him when he was in his living room or other parts of the magnificent property including the kitchen. This seemed reasonable to Ionna. She wouldn't want anyone wandering by and staring in at her.

'Thank you, I'd like to sketch the roses,' she accepted. 'I'll pop up this afternoon, if that's suitable.'

'It is. Feel free to wander around. The jasmine is blooming too, and the honeysuckle.'

'Ideal. I won't disturb you.'

His heart was unexpectedly disturbed right now just looking at her. And he was impressed that she hadn't rebuked him for the past. She'd become quite the confident young lady and career woman she'd set out to be when she left the village. Though he was well up on the gossip that she'd made a mess of things in Edinburgh and needed a sojourn to sort things out, including her book deadline. So essentially she was back because of her career, her business, not to flirt or have a summer fling with him.

Heat charged through his body, and smiling, he ran away, taking the fastest route back to the castle.

Ionna waited to see if he'd come back again, but when he didn't, she continued her sketches and then packed her bag and headed out of the forest. She needed a cup of tea, lunch soon, and to think of the pickle she was in danger of getting herself into. An afternoon at the castle's rose garden? She hadn't anticipated such an offer from the laird.

Emerging from the forest, she walked back across the fields and on to the coastal thoroughfare, breathing in the scent of the sea, and...was that freesias in Leith's front garden?

She walked across to his cottage and peered over the bramble hedging. Yes. And other flowers that interested her. The local soil was rich and Leith had cultivated a nice garden.

His van wasn't parked outside his cottage, so she rightly surmised he wasn't in. If she carefully stepped over the hedging for a minute she could take a few pictures of the flowers without disturbing anything.

Unfortunately, the hem of her dress got snagged on the brambles and while trying to pull it free, and not drop her bag, she took a tumble into his garden.

'I'd beat you at a hurdle race.' Leith's voice hit her harder than the soft landing on the recently cut lawn. He peered over at her sprawled on the grass, trying to pull her hem free.

His long legs stepped over the hedge and he lifted up the hem of her dress, without admiring her slender but shapely bare legs, and pulled it free of the jagged bramble hedging.

'I wasn't doing any harm,' she began, blushing and feeling flustered. And caught.

77

A strong hand reached down, clasped hers and pulled her up.

'I thought you were out...'

'I was, but I came back for a cup of tea and a sandwich.' He thumbed back towards the cottage he'd been working on. 'I left the van parked over there.'

Not thinking straight, she went to step back over the hedge to get out of his garden, but two strong hands this time clasped her by the waist and held her back. 'Hold on there. I do have a front gate. Or, you could come in for a cup of tea.'

Relieved that he wasn't snippy about her intruding, she took him up on his offer. Frankly, she was interested in having a peek inside his cottage. Had it changed? She hadn't been a regular visitor, but she remembered their last skirmish and wondered what his cottage looked like now.

'Okay,' she said, picking up her bag and following him inside. He hadn't even locked the front door.

Breezing through the hall, he led her to the kitchen. She noticed two tins of paint in the hall, and peeked into the living room as she walked by. He halted and gestured for her to take a look. She did, stepping into the traditional room with its comfortable furnishings.

Paint charts were on the table in front of the unlit fire. 'This will be nice when you've decorated the walls. Freshened up the icky cream.'

Leith swallowed his reaction as she picked up the paint charts and continued.

'This classic white would lift the whole atmosphere, make the room lighter and brighter.'

He took the charts off her. 'I painted the walls last week.'

'Oh!'

His finger tapped the colour chart. 'The shade is a warm cream.'

Ionna pressed her lips together.

'Say it, let it out,' he said.

'I just think the white would brighten the atmosphere. Look at the sunlight shining in. Picture how the living room would look light and airy.'

'The look is warm and homely.' He sounded as if that was the end of the colour conversation.

'You mentioned tea?' she prompted him.

He strode through to the kitchen and she followed, trying not to smirk when she saw that the freshly painted kitchen walls matched the living room.

Filling the kettle, he put it on to boil. Setting up the cups, he shot her a look.

She held up her hands. 'I'm saying nothing.'

Her expression said everything, and he found himself starting to smile.

'Can I help make the tea or your sandwiches?' she offered.

'No. You're in trouble magnet mode. Just sit down and don't mess with anything.'

She smiled sweetly, causing him to smile too.

Opening the fridge, he took out a block of Scottish cheddar cheese, butter, lettuce and tomatoes. 'I saw you earlier over in the field. I assumed you were working on your designs.'

'I was. I sketched thistles and took photos of them for crewelwork patterns. Then I went into the forest to find the bluebells.'

Leith washed his hands and prepared sandwiches for two. If she didn't want hers, he'd wrap them up and have them later.

Seeing the tasty sandwiches being made ignited her appetite. She washed her hands at the sink. Standing next to him, he towered over her and she was aware of his muscular stature. Again, his fresh scent reminded her of the sea.

Seeing Ionna in his kitchen threw his senses. How many times he'd pictured what it would be like to share his life with her, build a home together.

'Did you find the bluebells?'

'Yes, and pink versions too. They'll be gorgeous for the embroidery designs.' She stepped away from the sink, but let him see her steal a slice of cheese that he was cutting for the sandwiches. She laughed and popped it in her mouth.

'I bet Effy doesn't let you away with things like that.'

'Nooo, but you bring out another side of me sometimes.'

'The rascal side.'

'That'll do,' she said, accepting the label. 'Nice cheese, tangy and full of flavour.'

He cut another slice to replace the one she'd stolen and continued making the sandwiches.

'Can I have tomato pickle on my sandwich?' she said, noticing the various jars of condiments on a shelf and lifting the jar down. It looked like he hadn't yet opened it.

'Yes, bring it over. I'll open it.'

'I can manage. I have a knack for getting the tops off jars.' Gripping it tightly, she attempted her usual technique that worked so well the lid flew off the jar and some of the contents splattered across the front of Leith's top.

'Oops! Butter fingers.' She replaced the lid and put the jar on the table.

Leith took the top off and threw it in the wash basket. Standing there bare–chested wearing his jeans and boots, he took a deep breath and continued to make the sandwiches, adding tomato pickle to them.

'I seem to have a knack for getting you to take your tops off.'

Leith smirked and continued the conversation. 'Did you see anyone while you were in the forest?' He knew he shouldn't have said this, but...

Hesitation fronted her reply. 'I saw Roary on one of his runs.' True, but not the whole truth.

Leith put the sandwiches on two plates and started to make the tea as the kettle boiled.

'Did he stop to talk to you?' His back was towards her as he poured the tea, hiding his reaction when she told him what happened.

'He was polite. Welcomed me back to the village.'

'At least that's the ice broken.' Leith lifted two mugs of strong tea over to the table. 'Milk and sugar?'

'Just milk.'

Leith poured the milk into their mugs and sat down opposite her.

'He's invited me to sketch the flowers in the castle's rose garden.' She bit into her sandwich.

'Did you accept his invitation?'

With a mouthful of the sandwich, she nodded, hoping he wouldn't pry for details.

Leith tensed, but tried to look relaxed. 'When are you going?'

Ionna took a sip of her tea. 'This afternoon.'

His appetite vanished and he picked up his mug, cupping it in his hands. 'I didn't think he'd be so welcoming to you.'

'Neither did I. Life's just full of surprises. Look at us, having lunch in your freshly decorated kitchen talking about Roary, again.'

Leith didn't need reminded of their last conversation. The accusations, the argument that she was wasting her time with Roary. The laird didn't love her. Leith remembered calling her a fool and a troublemaker. The verbal skirmish had ended on a fiery note and been a harsh farewell.

'Let's talk about something else,' she said, smiling, encouraging him.

'What do you want to talk about?'

'Anything you want.'

'Okay, are you leaving the village when the summer's over?'

'Yes. I've no plans to stay.'

'Are you going to the ceilidh night at the hub?'

'I am. Effy and the other ladies from the crafting bee are all going.'

'Will you save a dance for me, if I go?'

'I will, if you do,' she promised.

Leith picked up his sandwich, feeling his appetite kick back into gear. 'Can I ask you something else?'

'Yes.'

'Was it always your dream to live in a fairytale castle?'

'No, not until I became enamoured with Roary. My fairytale was to live in a pretty cottage on a beautiful island in the Scottish Highlands, like the ones far off in the distance. I like the forest, but I've always loved the sea.'

They ate their lunch and chatted about the cottages Leith was refurbishing, and then Ionna picked up her bag. 'I'd better go now. Thanks for lunch.'

Leith put on a clean top. 'Come into the garden whenever you want to sketch the flowers and pick any you like.'

'I'd like to take pictures of the freesia.'

They walked outside. He didn't lock the door, and left Ionna to take photos of the freesia while he headed back to get on with the building work.

Checking the time, Ionna tucked her phone away when she had all the pictures she needed, and walked back across the fields and into the forest for her afternoon at the castle's rose garden.

Roary had showered and put on a pair of expensive black trousers and a white shirt. He'd skipped lunch, instructing Gorden to prepare a special afternoon tea.

Gorden was a robust man in his forties and wore his whites in the kitchen. 'What type of cake does Ionna prefer? Vanilla and cream sponge or chocolate cake?' he said to Roary.

'I don't know. Chocolate cake probably.'

Gorden looked unimpressed by Roary's reply.

Roary saw Donal walking by the kitchen window and waved him in urgently.

'Does Ionna prefer vanilla and cream sponge or chocolate cake for afternoon tea?' Roary said to Donal.

'I would think chocolate cake maybe,' Donal guessed.

Another glaring glance was issued by Gorden.

Donal sensed the urgency. 'I'll phone Effy. She'll know.'

Effy picked up.

Donal put the phone on speaker. 'What type of cake does Ionna like? Vanilla and cream sponge or chocolate cake?'

'Vanilla and cream,' Effy replied without hesitation, sensing Donal needed an instant reply.

Gorden noted this and bustled around the kitchen. He'd already baked a vanilla sponge cake that morning and it only needed the whipped cream. 'What type of scones does she like?' he called over to Donal.

Effy overheard Gorden. 'Plain scones with jam and cream.'

Gorden rustled up the scones while Donal finished the call to Effy.

'Why do you need to know?' Effy said to Donal.

'Roary is trying to impress her with a fancy afternoon tea at the castle,' Donal told her.

'I need you to give the roses a watering,' Roary said to Donal. 'Ionna will be here soon.'

'I have to go, Effy. Thanks for the information.' Donal clicked the call off. 'I'll give the roses a wee skoosh,' he said to Roary and then hurried out.

CHAPTER SEVEN

Sunlight shone through the canopy of trees near the heart of the forest. Ionna walked along one of the natural pathways, remembering the old routes she used to take when she was a wee girl, and as a young woman. The same sense of adventure she used to feel whenever she went meandering through it filled her with excitement.

There was always something about this forest and its hidden castle that instilled a sense of magical adventure. Bubbling under the surface. Filtering through the trees.

Shadows and light created an atmosphere of theatrical drama. She'd gone to a stage show in the city three years ago that was set in a forest. The stage scenery and lighting effects reminded her so much of this forest, hidden in the Highlands, that she'd felt such a sense of longing to be there again. Never thinking she would.

Effy had her shopping basket on her arm and paid for the fresh loaf, milk and vegetables in the wee shop. She'd told Jinnet that Ionna was having afternoon tea at the castle.

'Flirting with the laird!' Jinnet's tone was sharp. 'Silly lassie. It'll only end in tears again.'

'I don't know exactly what she's up to.' Effy added a bar of chocolate to her groceries. 'Ionna set out this morning all smiles to go looking for thistles in the fields.'

'She must've gone into the forest.'

Effy paid for the chocolate. 'Roary probably saw her. But why would he invite her to afternoon tea with him at the castle?'

'Maybe the laird's looking at her in a new light.'

'She had her blue chambray dress on. Her hair was freshly washed and she'd put on a wee bit of makeup. She looked lovely.'

'So it was Ionna that Leith lifted up in his garden a wee while ago,' Jinnet exclaimed. 'Ailish was in to buy flour to make scones for tonight's quilting bee. She said she saw Leith fooling around with a woman that was wearing a blue dress. Ailish couldn't see over the bramble hedging. She thinks Leith had her pinned on the lawn. Then he lifted her up and they went into his cottage. And closed the door. She noticed his van wasn't parked outside.'

Effy clutched at her cardigan. 'Oh, I was hoping Ionna was getting on with her embroidery designs, not fluttering around like a butterfly in Leith's garden and Roary's forest.'

'Don't worry, Effy,' Jinnet advised her. 'Ionna didn't seem like a wee minx last night. Mind you, she did arrive with Leith and he wasn't wearing his shirt.'

'That was because it got messed with the mud,' Effy said defensively, and then she remembered. 'Ionna was racing Leith late last night.' She told Jinnet the details. 'He was bare–chested again.'

Jinnet pursed her lips. 'We'll have to do something.'

'I'll phone Donal and tell him to stop her doing anything embarrassing.'

Donal wrestled with the garden hose, hurrying to water the roses before Ionna arrived.

'Hello, Donal. The roses are looking beautiful.'

He turned at the sound of Ionna's voice. 'I'm just giving them a wee skoosh of water.' Donal continued to tussle with the hose, getting himself into a fankle in his rush to finish.

'Let me help you unravel that,' Ionna offered, putting her bag down on the grass. 'I have a knack for getting knots out of thread and wool. I can see where the hose is twisted.' Without waiting for Donal to agree, she pulled the hose from him. 'It's twirled in the middle. I'll just—'

Flipping the hose and giving it a hard pull, her helpful intentions sprayed the water in all directions. 'It's fine, I've got it under control,' she said.

Donal ran away to turn the water off at the source, leaving Ionna wrestling with the hose. The water sprayed on the roses so no damage was done until she decided to water the climbing roses on the archway as Roary stepped through it wondering what all the commotion was.

His white shirt was soaked in seconds. The wet fabric clung to every contour of his chest and shoulders and dripped from his hair.

Ionna gasped, a second before Donal turned the water off and came hurrying back.

'That's it off,' Donal shouted, and then jolted when he saw the laird standing there drenched.

Ionna dropped the hose and bit her lip. Had the welcome to the castle mat just been ripped out from under her feet?

'Afternoon tea is ready!' Gorden only saw the rear view of the laird as he called to them from the kitchen door. Unaware of the predicament, he prepared to serve their tea outside on the patio.

Should she run, or stay? Ionna wasn't sure. She'd yet to see Roary smile since they'd become reacquainted. And he certainly wasn't smiling now.

'Donal's not answering his phone,' Effy said to Jinnet.

'He'll be tending to something urgent at the estate. Leave a message,' said Jinnet.

Effy's phone rang.

'Were you trying to phone me?' Donal whispered, not wanting the laird or Ionna to overhear him.

'Yes, I'm worried that Ionna will create a fuss at the castle. Could you herd off any trouble she could cause?'

'Too late, Effy. Roary's taking his shirt off in the garden as we speak.' Donal told her what was happening.

As his shirt was soaking wet, Roary didn't want to make a mess of the castle's tartan carpeting when he went inside to get changed into dry clothes.

'I'll won't be long,' Roary said to Ionna. 'Have a look around the garden, and then we'll have afternoon tea.' He didn't seem upset with her, so she smiled as he hurried inside.

'So everything is fine, Effy,' Donal assured her, finishing the call.

'Does Effy know what happened?' Ionna said to Donal.

'She does, but I explained it was a fankled hose. I'm sure Roary won't be long. Have a wee donner around the rose garden.'

The scent of the roses filled the air with a heady fragrance, and Ionna took photos of the roses. And she included pictures of the magnificent castle.

The castle was set in the heart of the forest with spacious gardens surrounding the historic structure with its ornate turrets. The private residence was well looked after by the laird, and he'd retained as much of the original elements as he could while keeping the building maintained.

Ionna imagined this is how it would've looked decades ago, and she loved the sense of grandeur it portrayed.

Roary had run upstairs to his bedroom, threw the wet shirt aside, and took off his trousers that had been splashed with water.

The room was classic luxury with a double bed, decorated in muted tones and had a wonderful view of the forest. Two books he'd been reading were on his bedside table.

Opening up his wardrobe, he grabbed another white shirt and dark trousers, put them on and looked at himself in the mirror to see that he was presentable again. Running his hands through his thick dark hair, he pushed the wet strands back from his face, and then hurried back downstairs to join Ionna.

Effy was still talking to Jinnet in the shop.

'I feel better knowing Ionna has only gone there to sketch the roses and flowers. Though it sounds like Roary is trying to impress her inviting her to have afternoon tea.'

'Nothing wrong with that,' said Jinnet. 'As long as she keeps things nice and friendly, but not too friendly.'

Leith walked in to buy a bottle of cold lemonade to refresh himself while doing the building work.

Two sets of disapproving eyes stared at him as he opened the fridge and helped himself to a bottle. He put it down on the counter and frowned at Effy and Jinnet.

'Am I interrupting something? If you're gossiping, I just want a bottle of lemonade.' He went to pay for it, but Effy told him bluntly what was wrong.

'There's gossip circulating that you had Ionna pinned down on your front lawn and then you whisked her into your cottage.'

He smiled, knowing how the village gossip could become whipped up over nothing. Taking a moment he summarised what really happened. The ladies commented as he explained.

'Her dress got caught on the bramble hedging?' said Effy.

'Freesia flowers are pretty,' Jinnet remarked.

'Your van was parked at the other cottage?' Effy realised.

'Icky cream paint?' Even Jinnet didn't like the sound of that.

'Tomato pickle?' Effy started to join the dots the right way.

'So nothing scandalous happened,' Leith concluded, having elaborated that yes, he had taken his stained top off, but then they ate their sandwiches and went their separate ways.

'Ionna's having afternoon tea with Roary at the castle,' said Effy.

'I know,' Leith confirmed. 'That's where she was heading when she left my cottage.'

They told him about the soaking the laird received from the hose water.

'The only knack that Ionna seems to have is for getting men to take their clothes off,' Leith concluded.

Bhictoria walked into the full blast of Leith's remark.

'Is this a bad time?' said Bhictoria. 'I'm only popping in for custard powder. We've run out of it. Trifles are on the hub's summer menu. Brochan's busy melting the raspberry jelly.'

'I was just leaving,' Leith said to Bhictoria. 'The ladies will tell you the latest gossip.'

Leith left and the gossiping began.

'Will we have tea on the patio?' Roary gestured to Ionna to join him. He made no mention of the furore she'd caused, and the pleasantries began as he seated her at the garden table. Gorden had set it with white linen and silverware. Roary sat down opposite Ionna.

Gorden's silver trolley rattled as he pushed it out of the kitchen and served up the delicious selection of cakes, scones and tea. And then he disappeared into the kitchen to let them enjoy themselves.

Roary poured their tea. 'I have your three embroidery books in the castle's library,' he revealed.

'Really?' Ionna sounded surprised.

'Effy gifted me one each time it was published,' he explained. 'It seemed appropriate to add the editions to the castle's library. After all, you were born and raised in the village. It's fitting that you're part of the library's history.'

'I'm truly taken aback. And delighted. Effy didn't tell me.'

'Unless I'm wrong, I hear that you hadn't kept in touch after you moved to Edinburgh.'

'You're correct, but I aim to keep in contact when I go back to the city.'

'Tell me about your new book. Donal says you've got a tight deadline to finish it.'

'Yes, so I'm hoping that being here in the village, amid all this beautiful scenery will help me design patterns with a floral and nature theme.'

'Feel free to pop up to the castle's garden and the forest to sketch your designs. I trust the roses will be useful for your patterns.'

'The roses are perfect. And the bluebells. I'll certainly include all of these in my new book.'

'I'll buy a copy for the library. And any others you create.'

'I've signed another three–book deal with my publishers,' she said.

'After our tea, I'll show you the library.'

They continued chatting and Ionna helped herself to a slice of the vanilla cream sponge and a scone with jam and cream.

Roary found himself admiring Ionna, her smiling face, the cheery and polite conversation discussing the village, the castle, books, gardens and flowers. Sunshine highlighted her silky blonde hair and he'd forgotten how her eyes were an incredible shade of violet–blue.

The sharpness of his past behaviour towards her was like a dagger in his heart. He'd grown up a lot since then, but that was no excuse. No wonder she left the village.

'...and I plan to include an artistic version of Effy's cottage in my embroidery patterns,' Ionna told him.

Roary knew the people that owned all the local cottages, but he'd hardly been inside any of the properties.

He put his napkin down on the table. 'Come on, I'll give you a whirlwind tour of the castle and then show you the copies of your books.'

Ionna stood up and let him escort her through the patio doors that led into the function room.

She stopped to admire an oil painting of the castle from the past. 'The castle still looks like it did all those years ago.'

'I try to maintain the structure and decor rather than replace and modernise it. Some upgrading has been done, but in a subtle way that doesn't jar with the original architecture.'

He surmised her thoughts from her expression having seen many others wonder the same things. 'The upkeep is expensive, but the estate functions on a profit and I supplement it through my regular business trips. Investments, those sort of financial dealings.'

He led her through the function room into the grand hallway.

'I read the feature of you in the magazine. The one where you're on the cover. It said that you're determined not to make the castle into a hotel.'

'That's right. If I have to one day, I will, rather than let it crumble. But it's not necessary at the moment, so I aim to keep it private. I value my privacy and so far the castle is well–managed by myself and the staff.'

'If this system is working for you, don't mess with it. I don't have a castle or anything grand, but I've meddled with things that I should've left well alone and later regretted it.'

She'd left the village, and him, he thought.

He stopped at the bottom of the plush carpeted staircase. As tall as Leith, he gazed down at her.

'Do you regret leaving the village?'

'No.' Her reply was instant. 'That was the right move for me under the circumstances.'

Neither of them brought up the topic of her having had a crush on him.

Roary led her upstairs. 'What about the current circumstances? Things change, people change.'

'I'm planning to work on my book, relax, join in with the local crafting bee, find my true north.'

At the top of the stairs was a large window overlooking the forest and countryside. Roary stopped to show her the view. 'This is one of my favourite views from the castle. Lights glow from the main street, and the farmhouses and cottages all around.'

'I can imagine it's magical. Last night I went down the shore and the sky was so clear and sparkling with stars.'

'Your Aunt Effy must be happy you're home.'

'She is. I'd mistakenly let our contact drift. But that's on me.'

Ionna had never been upstairs in the castle, but glancing round she noticed what she rightly assumed was Roary's bedroom. The door was open wide and she could see the double bed and the white shirt cast on the floor where he'd thrown it. Deliberately turning to look away, she kept the conversation light.

'It's a wonderful view,' she said, gazing out over the forest.

Roary had no intention to entice her into his bedroom, but realised him taking her upstairs could be construed as such. He gestured to the real reason he'd brought her there. Near the window was an original oil painting.

'I thought you'd be interested in seeing this,' he said.

Ionna stood beside him.

'This was painted a long time ago. It shows the village from the past and you can see the little white cottages down near the sea.'

Ionna peered at the details of the tiny cottages depicted in the local landscape painting. The scene was mainly sea, forest and fields, but the whitewashed cottages had been included.

'That must be Effy's cottage.' She stepped closer to study the artwork. 'Yes, if that's Leith's cottage there, Effy's is this one.' Her smile warmed Roary's heart as she looked at him, delighted to see a glimpse of the historic past.

'When you mentioned that you planned to embroider Effy's cottage, I thought you'd like this.'

'Thank you for showing me the painting.'

'Let's go downstairs to the living room,' he said.

They walked down the wide staircase together and he led her into his private room that had a library area in the far corner. The top shelves were so high a ladder was needed to reach the upper books. The lower levels were filled with a selection of fiction and non–fiction books, some so old that they were worth a small fortune, but the laird had no intention of parting with them.

'And these are your three embroidery books.' Roary reached over and lifted the books from a shelf. Other non–fiction titles bookended them.

Immaculate, they looked like they'd never been opened, and certainly not used.

'I admit that I haven't studied them.' Roary went over to his desk and came back with a pen and handed it to her. 'Would you sign them?'

Ionna had attended a couple of events that her publishers had organised to promote her books when they were launched. More book publicity and promos were planned. Opening the first book, she signed her name on the title page. And then did the same for the other two.

She handed the books to him. He opened one and looked at her signature, then placed all three back on the shelf.

'Did you ever learn to play chess?' he said, seeing her notice the chess board on the table beside his favourite armchair. He remembered her saying she intended to learn. At the time he thought it was another ploy to gain his attention.

'I never did. Once I was in Edinburgh, I had neither the time or inclination. I don't think chess is for me. I'm happy with my embroidery and crafting.'

He wasn't sure if he was disappointed. But it was refreshing to have the company of someone unwilling to say all the right things to impress or beguile him. And off all the women, it was Ionna.

CHAPTER EIGHT

Ionna sat on a bench in the castle's garden sketching the roses and other flowers. Roary was in his living room letting her get on with her artwork.

She sketched the pink tea roses, picturing how she'd use long and short stitches to create the colour gradation of the petals. This would be one of the larger designs in her book, and she included the details of the flowers. Opening a box of artists coloured pencils, she used various shades of pink and green to create the artwork.

The bright sunlight started to give way to an amber glow as the afternoon wore on, and Ionna packed up her sketch pad and pencils and went over to talk to Donal.

'I'm heading home now,' she said. The laird was nowhere to be seen.

'Roary's inside on a business call.'

'Don't disturb him. But tell him thanks later.' Ionna walked away, heading back into the forest.

The amber sunlight of the late afternoon shone through the trees creating an atmosphere that felt like being in an oil painting from the past. The burnished tones and rich textures of the forest made the designer in her picture colour combinations and the types of threads she'd use for her patterns.

She hadn't gone far when a voice called out.

'Ionna!'

She stopped and looked round to see Roary running after her.

'I was going to give you a lift back down to the village,' he said, not at all out of breath.

'It's fine. I enjoy walking, and it's such a nice afternoon.'

'I'll walk with you.'

They fell into an easy step together.

'Will you be working on your designs this evening?' he said.

'No, I'm going to a quilting bee night at Ailish's cottage.'

'So you're a quilter as well as an embroiderer.'

'Embroidery is my main craft, but I love all sorts of sewing and knitting. The crafting bee nights are like social evenings and the members are welcome to work on whatever craft they want. I'm taking my quilting and my embroidery with me. Though I'll probably chatter and gossip as much as I craft.'

'I hear that Ailish has built up her quilting business from her cottage.'

'Yes. Several of the crafting bee members are doing well selling items on their websites, including Effy. She says the online sales of her embroidery, quilts and knitting keeps her busy with orders.'

'Anything else you notice that's changed since you came back?'

'Surprisingly, very little. There was always something going on in the village, and that doesn't seem to have changed. I haven't been to the shops in the main street yet. But I here that Brochan and Bhictoria's hub has a new extension built months ago. She told me they've extended the function room at the back of the bar. It now has a bigger floor for the ceilidh dances. I'll see it soon when I go to the next ceilidh night.'

'Donal mentioned about the hub's extension, but I haven't seen it. I've been away a lot on business.'

It didn't sound like an excuse, and Ionna knew that the laird didn't frequent the local hub.

They walked on.

'I notice you're not wearing a wedding ring,' he said boldly.

'I'm not married. I just came out of a messy relationship. My ex–boyfriend is in Edinburgh. We won't be getting back together.'

Roary didn't pry for the details.

'What about you?' she said.

'Single. No girlfriend. I date, mainly when I'm away.'

'I'm happy with my career, for the moment,' she told him.

'The business trips take me away from the castle a lot, but I'm aiming to cut down on my travels and become more settled in the village.'

'I don't see myself settling here, though I've only just arrived.'

'You've got the whole summer to see if you'd feel at home again in the village. Maybe you'll find that some things have changed for the better.'

She looked around. 'The forest hasn't changed. It's still feels as hidden and magical as ever.'

Tree roots formed a gnarled path down through the heart of the forest. Ionna stepped carefully, remembering this was the fastest route to take.

A strong hand gripped hers and held her steady, taking the lead.

The touch of his hand sent a shock through her system, feeling his elegant fingers wrap around hers. In all the years she'd had a crush on him, this was the first time she'd ever held his hand. Roary had invariably kept his distance, even at the balls at the castle.

Neither of them said anything, and she didn't pull away. She imagined that to an onlooker they would seem like a romantic couple strolling hand in hand through the forest. How strange, she thought, that she used to dream of one day doing this. Now here she was, but it didn't feel the way she'd imagined. Something in her jarred, as if she was trying to settle the past and make it fit the present.

Thinking so deeply, she lost concentration and stepped on a tree root that caused her to stumble. She would've fallen if Roary hadn't been there. From one strong hand, she now had two strong arms lifting her up and carrying her down the remainder of the way.

For some reason, this made her laugh, nerves probably or a long–held dream finally coming true.

Her fingers felt the lean muscles underneath the fabric of his shirt. She'd hooked her bag on one arm and put her other arm around his shoulder.

Roary carried her with ease as he made his way down the gnarled path towards the bluebells.

'I think you can safely put me down now,' she said, smiling.

'Almost there. The roots could trip you up. You could take a tumble and sprain your ankle in those shoes. I don't want to be responsible for ruining your visit here. You'll want to be fit for the ceilidh dancing.'

Keeping her arms around him, she leaned back a little and studied his face. 'You've changed.'

The intense green eyes gazed at her. 'For the better?'

'I think so.'

'But you're not sure.'

'You barely acknowledged me in the past. Now here you are being chivalrous, like I imagined a laird of a castle should be.'

'That sounds better to me.'

'But why the change of tune?'

'A change of heart,' he said. 'Seeing you again. We've both grown up.'

Ionna cheekily reached up and ran her hand through the tree blossoms, causing the petals to fall on them.

Sensing she was in a playful mood, Roary, whirled her around as they reached the bluebells.

Ionna's laughter resonated through the forest. 'No, Roary!'

Leith had no business walking across the fields to the forest. But he couldn't help himself. While finishing the building work for the day, he kept thinking about Ionna having afternoon tea with the laird. He'd tried to concentrate on the work, but his senses were urging him to do something. But what?

He couldn't very well invite himself to tea, not that he'd be welcomed by Roary. And Ionna was there to sketch flowers.

But like his recent dreams of a storm, his senses warned him that trouble was brewing. Roary had shown no romantic interest in Ionna before, but would the laird now see her for the beautiful young woman she'd become? And in Leith's eyes, always was.

Packing his tools away, he left the van parked at the cottage he'd been working on and strode across the fields. He didn't expect to see either of them, and yet...his instincts made him walk towards the gap in the trees where he'd entered the forest before many times, just for a wander like others living locally.

As he stepped under the branches into the forest the sound of Ionna's laughter filtered through the air. And then he saw her, swept up in Roary's arms, and their playful behaviour. The dagger through his heart was an unexpected wound he wasn't ready for.

They were so wrapped up in each other they didn't even notice him watching them for a moment.

And then Leith turned around and hurried away, out of the forest, back across the fields, unpacked his tools, picked up his hammer and began working again on the cottage extension. His stomach was knotted and he couldn't bare thinking what the two of them were up to now.

The laird wasn't the type to flirt with the local lassies, so his interest in Ionna was obvious. And no wonder. She'd become even lovelier than when she left. They'd probably enjoyed tea and cakes outside on the castle's patio or served up inside, all silverware and sparkling chandeliers.

Muttering to himself for having given in to his instincts, he concentrated on the extension work.

Climbing up his ladder, he looked out over the shore. The turquoise sea gave no hint of a storm, but in the distance, grey clouds were beginning to shield the amber glow of the fading afternoon sun, indicating that a storm was on its way.

Ionna emerged from the forest and walked across the fields, heading back home to Effy's cottage.

In the distance, she saw the familiar figure up a ladder, working on one of the cottages. Her heart reacted, seeing Leith, working hard, looking fit and strong. His auburn hair matched the fiery amber glow of the sun, though there were grey clouds sweeping in towards the coast. Hopefully, the storm would blow by, like they often did. But would the feeling in her heart? An unfamiliar sadness mixed with longing.

Putting her reaction down to the topsy–turvy day, she walked on, but the path through the fields took her closer to Leith.

Sensing he was being watched, Leith glanced round, still perched on the ladder, and saw Ionna in the distance. Pretending he hadn't noticed her, he made a big show of his hammering.

Unsure whether he'd seen her or not, Ionna continued on home. She wouldn't have known what to say to Leith anyway. Tell him she'd had a nice afternoon at the castle and sketched roses? This was true. But would she tell him that Roary had lifted her up and flirted with her?

Suddenly feeling the need to get home where she couldn't cause any more trouble for herself, she ran the rest of the way.

Leith saw her running all the way to Effy's cottage and disappearing inside.

Effy felt the rush of air from the hallway as Ionna hurried in and closed the door firmly, shutting out the mischief she'd caused.

The cottage smelled of raspberry jelly.

Ionna put her bag down on the hall table and went through to the kitchen to find Effy stirring raspberry jelly in a glass bowl.

'Bhictoria mentioned trifle when I was in the wee shop. It put me in the mood to make a trifle.'

Whatever mood Ionna had tried to shut out changed the homely atmosphere in the kitchen, weighing it down. Effy stopped stirring the melting jelly. 'I know that you soaked the laird with water, if that's what's bothering you. Donal told me all about it.'

The atmosphere remained heavy, and Ionna's expression showed she was upset.

'What else happened?' said Effy.

In a burst of chatter Ionna summarised the salient issues. 'And I think Leith pretended he hadn't seen me when I came out of the forest a few minutes ago.'

'I don't blame him. It was tempting trouble going up to the castle. You should know that.'

Ionna didn't argue. 'Leith must've seen us. Maybe he had a view through the trees when he was up the ladder. I think he gave me the cold shoulder, and I can only surmise it was because he saw Roary lifting me up and us laughing like we were...'

'A couple?' Effy finished for her.

'If I could rewind, I would've told Roary to put me down. I wouldn't have accepted his invitation to afternoon tea. I would've sketched the thistles in the field this morning and not gone into the forest in search of the bluebells.'

Effy put the bowl of jelly aside to cool. 'What are you going to do?'

Ionna slumped down on a kitchen chair. 'Hide here in the cottage and get on with my embroidery patterns.'

'Oh, no you're not!' Effy took a firm stance. 'You didn't come all the way here from Edinburgh to hide. I've been looking forward to you visiting for the summer. So you can forget about hiding. I'm not having that in this house.'

Ionna blinked, taken aback, but she could see that Effy was adamant as she continued.

'I knew you'd still be a magnet for trouble. I just didn't think you'd cause it so fast. But here's what you're going to do. You're coming with me to Ailish's quilting bee tonight. And you'll paste on a smile if you have to, but you're going with all of the bee ladies to the ceilidh at the hub. So wash your hands, put an apron on, and start whipping up the buttercream icing for the butterfly cakes.'

Effy gestured to the tray of vanilla cupcakes she'd baked to take to the quilting bee. She started to slice the tops off to make the sponge wings ready to be stuck on top with the buttercream.

Feeling suddenly better, Ionna washed her hands at the sink, dried them and put on a pretty apron that was hanging up.

'I took the butter out of the fridge to soften it,' said Effy, setting the cakes on a tray. 'Do you remember how much sugar to add when you're whipping it?'

'Yes.' Butterfly cakes were one of the first things she'd learned to bake when she was a wee girl. Effy had taught her many skills. Now she was gaining a lesson in facing up to things instead of hiding.

'Roary's certainly got an appetite for his dinner tonight,' Gorden confided to Donal. 'Steak pie and tatties, then plum duff and custard.'

Donal was eating a spare portion of this in the kitchen. He often ate his meals at the castle kitchen, especially when he was working late.

'I think a young lady has sparked his appetite,' said Donal, enjoying the pie with lashings of rich gravy.

'Aye, and for more than his dinner.' Gorden sat down at the table and drank a large mug of tea.

'I hear they were fooling around in the forest,' Donal revealed. 'One of the staff saw them.'

'There are no secrets around here.'

'I'm phoning the girls to tell them the gossip before we go to Ailish's bee night.' Effy picked up her phone. 'It's better to bring things out into the open rather than let folk spread whispers and blow everything out of proportion.'

Ionna was packing the butterfly cakes into a large biscuit tin to carry them to Ailish's cottage. 'I don't want to spoil the quilting bee.'

'That's why I'm phoning to air the situation. The ladies have a few wee surprises for you.'

'What are they?'

'You'll find out later. Now away through and get your craft bag ready while I talk about you behind your back.'

Ionna managed to laugh and left Effy to make the calls.

Ailish's cottage was nearby. The front door was open in welcoming and a few of the ladies made their way inside, including Ionna and Effy.

Ailish had set up her living room with folding chairs and a couple of tables. While her parents were away for the year, Ailish had allowed her quilting business to spill over from her own room at the back of the cottage into the living room.

Neatly folded piles of quilting weight cotton fabric were on the shelves of an old–fashioned dresser. This was where Ailish kept her fabric stash. It included pre–cut bundles of fabric in prints and solid colours. Beside the dresser were craft boxes filled with off–cuts of fabric, scraps that were used for patchwork and making hexies for quilts.

Quilted cushions, made by Ailish, added comfort to the chairs and although nothing matched, the whole eclectic mix of designs created a haven that Ionna liked as soon as she walked into the living room.

A few knowing glances were exchanged by the ladies as they settled themselves. The gossip had been aired and no mention of Ionna's flirting with the laird was cast up. Ionna was the focus of their attention. But it had nothing to do with the romantic ructions.

Effy added the tin of butterfly cakes to the scones Ailish had baked, and the tasty items the others had brought with them.

Ionna hung her craft bag on the back of a seat and went to sit down.

'No, don't sit down yet, Ionna.' Ailish lifted up a measuring tape. 'Come over so we can measure you for the patterns.'

'What patterns?' said Ionna.

Mairead held up a dress pattern. 'This one, for a start.' She showed Ionna the picture of a classic shift dress on the front of the pattern.

'Hands out so I can measure your waist,' Ailish told Ionna. She read out the measurements and three of the ladies noted them down.

'What's going on?' Ionna said with an excited smile.

'We're taking the short course in filling your wardrobe with dresses and skirts you can wear for the summer,' Mairead explained.

Vaila unpacked a ditsy print dress from her a bag. 'I wore this once on a knitwear modelling shoot. I've never worn it since. I'm sure it'll fit you.'

'Try this skirt on too,' Jinnet added. 'It's a light denim wrap skirt. I washed it today. I've only worn it a few times. I thought it would tide you over while you restock your wardrobe with vintage pieces and other clothes.'

'You said you practically live in jeans and don't have many dresses left,' said Effy. 'There's nothing much in your wardrobe except the three dresses I kept, and you can't keep wearing them all the time.'

'I was going to start buying vintage pieces online,' said Ionna.

'We know,' said Effy. 'But this will give you a head start. A basic wardrobe you can build on.'

Bhictoria had brought a wrap tea dress with a rose print and held it up. 'Yes, this will be pretty on you. I made it last summer. You're welcome to have it.'

The surprise was nothing like what she'd expected. Kindness and generosity personified. And all she'd done was cause trouble. A huge wave of emotion swept over Ionna and she blinked away the tears.

'Don't upset yourself, lass.' Effy gave her niece a reassuring smile.

'Thank you,' Ionna said, sniffing back the tears and taking a deep breath. 'You're all so kind.'

'The kettle's on for tea,' said Ailish. 'Have a look through the fabrics and see what you'd like for dresses and skirts.'

'I don't want to take up your time dressmaking for me,' said Ionna.

Mairead stepped forward holding the pattern. 'I'll have this pattern cut out before the night's done. Then I'll machine it tomorrow. It'll be ready by tomorrow evening.' Mairead was an expert dressmaker and no one contradicted her.

111

Another two ladies were seamstresses and most of the ladies had made their own clothes or altered items before.

Gathering around Ionna, they took measurements, preferences for hem lengths, the type of sleeves and bodice styles. They helped Ionna select fabrics she liked but advised on the type of prints that would suit her.

Then the tea, cakes and scones were served up, along with plenty of local gossip, tactfully avoiding any mention of Ionna's antics.

Surrounded by cheery chatter and crafting, Ionna felt her predicament drift into proper perspective. No hiding. No more nonsense. Tomorrow, she'd start the day afresh.

Leith couldn't settle. Even after working a full day, and into the evening decorating the spare bedroom in his cottage, he wasn't tired enough to relax let alone fall asleep.

He went outside into the garden and breathed in the fresh air wafting up from the sea. The storm hadn't arrived yet. The grey clouds lingered over the distant islands. The sea was calm and he decided to go for a swim.

Leith changed into a pair of red trunks, deck shoes, threw a large white towel around his shoulders and headed down to the shore. There was no one around. He had it all to himself.

'I won't be long,' Ionna assured Effy. 'It was such a great night at the quilting bee. I'm so excited about the dresses and skirts. I'd like to take a wee walk down to the shore to unwind and then come back and get to bed.'

'Okay.' Effy put the empty tin in the kitchen. The butterfly cakes had gone down a treat. 'I'm going to get ready for my bed.'

'I promise I won't be up to mischief or any silly adventures. I'll even use the front door.'

'If I'm sleeping by the time you get back, climb in the windae.'

Ionna laughed and headed outside and down to the sea that shimmered in the nightglow.

CHAPTER NINE

Leith kicked off his shoes and walked down on to the sand. The sea sparkled under a night sky that hadn't decided if it would release a thunder storm later or breeze by without a ripple.

The sand felt soothing underneath his bare feet, relieving the tension in him before he even went into the water. The sea lapped gently on to the shore and he walked towards it, threw his towel down, waded in and dived under.

His usual route was to swim along the coast, using the light shining from his cottage as a navigation beacon. He'd been swimming there since he was a boy and was a strong and capable swimmer.

In the dark sea he soon became part of the scenery.

Ionna took a deep breath of sea air as she walked down on to the sand. Seeing something white lying near the edge of the water, she went over and picked up the white towel. Thinking someone had forgotten to take it home with them from earlier, she folded it and walked back up and put it down where the owner would see it in the morning. Left overnight, it would get washed out to sea.

Heading back down, she stood facing the sea, breathing in the calming air for a few minutes.

Leith headed back, using the light beacon to keep him on course. The swim helped ease the tension in his muscles, but his mind kept rewinding the scene in the forest with Ionna and Roary. He could still hear her laughter.

On the last straight, he powered through the water and then stood up and waded out.

Ionna jumped seeing Leith suddenly emerge from the sea.

He blinked the sea water from his eyes and swept his hair back from his surprised face.

Don't run, she urged herself.

'Going in for a dook?' He stood thigh deep in the sea, and spoke in a tone that challenged her.

'No, taking in the sea air to unwind before heading back to get some sleep.'

'Ah, yes, you've had such an exciting day.' He started to walk out of the sea, all rippling wet muscles and raw masculinity.

She pretended not to be affected by the rivulets of water running over the lean muscles of his chest, or the soaking wet red trunks that left little to the imagination.

He continued to close the gap between them and within moments his tall physique was a broad shouldered silhouette shielding her view of the sea.

'I suppose the white towel I found discarded on the sand belongs to you.'

He stepped closer still. 'Where did you hide it?'

'I didn't hide it. I put it up near the road so it wouldn't get washed out to sea.'

With no towel to drape around himself, Leith stood there dripping wet, looking down at her.

'Did you enjoy your afternoon tea at the castle?' He sounded as if he was holding back what he really wanted to talk about.

'Yes, it was nice.'

'I expect you'll be invited to dinner there next.' The bitterness in his tone was evident. 'You and the laird seem to have patched up your differences.'

He had seen them fooling around in the forest! She could tell from the bile burning in him.

'Were you watching me today when the laird was walking me home through the forest?' Her words were clear, challenging. 'I saw you perched up a ladder. I assume you had a great view.'

The broad shoulders jolted and he adjusted his stance to become even bolder. 'I saw you because I went into the forest,' he clarified. 'You weren't walking. Roary had you in his arms, lifting you up. You were laughing, having fun.'

'Nothing happened.'

'Just flirting with the laird.' He put it so succinct, but he was right.

'I wish I hadn't gone to the castle, or the forest. Roary was flirting with me, and I...'

'Encouraged him.'

'People make mistakes,' she said defensively.

'I made one six years ago. The day you left. I still relive it. I won't be repeating that one again.'

Ionna looked up at him as he continued.

'I kept my mouth shut. Well, I'm speaking up now, Ionna.'

'I can't change the past,' she said.

'No, but you seem to be repeating it.'

'The crush I had on Roary was a long time ago. I don't have those feelings for him now. And you seem like you're doing okay for yourself.'

'Am I? I'm still remembering the birthday every year of a woman that never cared for me.'

'My birthday?'

'Happy birthday from last week,' he said.

Her heart was pounding. 'What am I supposed to do? I came back to work on my book.'

Leith moved so close she thought he was going to take her in his strong arms and kiss the breath from her. Or maybe this was what she secretly wanted, or needed.

He had been tempted but instead he spoke up. 'You need to unravel yourself from whatever hurt, heartache and nonsense you've brought with you from Edinburgh. I'm going to be busy. I plan to finish the main exterior building work in the next two weeks. Then I'll be working inside the cottages on the interior alterations and decor.'

'Fine. I'll be designing the embroidery patterns for my book.'

His blue eyes glanced at her as he walked away, as if he wouldn't see her for a while.

An empty feeling jarred her, but she stood where she was, gazing out at the sea. Then temptation made her look round at the tall retreating figure pick up his towel, throw it around his shoulders, put his shoes on and walk into the shadows of the night.

Ionna looked at the sea again. Upset, rewinding the things Leith had said to her, and how close he was to summing up her situation. Thinking that he'd remembered her birthday every year from a silent distance. She'd never known about that.

Glancing round again, she noticed more lights were shining from the windows of Leith's cottage. He was probably showering off the sea water.

She immediately blinked away the image that accompanied this thought. His lean–muscled body wearing the wet trunks was already etched in her mind, invoking feelings she didn't want to admit to. Leith was a looker, and most women would react in a similar manner she assured herself.

A gust of wind blew in from the sea, and she swept her hair back as she heard the low rumble of distant thunder.

Moments later, a flash of lightning lit up the sky.

She should've hurried back to the cottage, but she didn't. Feeling the energy of the approaching storm, she breathed it in and took out her phone to take a photograph of the way the far off islands were aglow as the lightning lit them up.

Leith stepped out of the shower, initially unaware of the approaching storm. As he padded through to his bedroom, drying himself off, he heard the thunder.

The lightning suddenly lit up his darkened bedroom as he got ready for bed with the lights off, using the nightglow shining in from outside to illuminate the room.

Gazing out the window, he saw the fast–moving clouds against the dark sky. A storm was on its way this time. He'd seen too many like this to be wrong.

And there, still standing down on the shore, was the little blonde figure watching the storm.

Rain hit off the window, and he saw Ionna make a bolt for home, running against the wind before the approaching downpour drenched her.

Throwing aside the jeans he'd grabbed ready to dash down and tell her to run for cover, he got into bed and watched the rain patter against the window, drumming a steady rhythm.

Ionna ran back to the cottage and climbed in her bedroom window. The lights were off in Effy's room and she used her favourite route so as not to wake her.

Her dress was spattered with rain and she hung it up on the outside of the wardrobe to dry.

Peeking in the wardrobe, she smiled when she saw the dresses and skirts the crafting bee ladies had given her. Her clothes were starting to look like the pre–loved and vintage fashions she used to wear. Effy intended making her a dress from the patterns in her folder. It felt like she was off–loading the past, bit by bit, starting with being here in the village, and wearing clothes that she loved.

Towel drying her hair and putting on a nightie, she stood for a few moments looking out the window at the rain sweeping in from the sea and battering against the glass. Storms like this usually blew past by the morning.

She got into bed and pulled the quilt up, feeling safe and cosy tucked up in the cottage.

Thinking about her recent encounter with Leith, she tried not to dwell on rewinding him striding out of the sea, or standing so close to her, causing her heart to react.

A few of the things he'd said made it clear that he was going to be busy. She was too. In the morning she planned to work on her designs and keep out of mischief.

'Do you want share of the porridge, or would you prefer toast?' said Effy as Ionna went through for breakfast wearing the vintage denim wrap skirt Jinnet had given her, and a light blue top.

'Porridge please.'

Effy poured it into their bowls and added creamy milk.

A pot of tea was on the table.

They sat down to have their breakfast and chat about their plans for the day.

'I'm going to make a start on the dress I promised you,' said Effy. 'And I notice you're wearing the denim skirt Jinnet gave you.'

'It's comfy and I love vintage denim.'

'That was some storm last night. Did you get caught in the rain when you were down the shore?'

'A wee bit. I ran back to the cottage when it started and missed the worst of the rain.' She looked out the kitchen window and saw that the sun was trying to burn away the remainder of the grey clouds. Then she told Effy what happened with Leith.

Effy laughed. 'That man is wearing less nearly every time you meet him. A pair of soaking wet swimming trunks! What next? A bare bahookie?'

This made Ionna laugh, lightening the conversation. She poured two cups of tea. 'He says he's going to be busy with his building work the next two weeks. I told him I intend to work on my patterns.'

'It'll give you time to settle in, and let you get on with your book.'

'Would it be okay if I set up my light box at the table near the window in the living room?'

'Yes, I'll be cutting the pattern and running the dress up with my sewing machine. Unless that will disturb your work.'

'Not at all. It'll be like before when we used to embroider and sew in the living room.'

Effy cleared the porridge bowls away and Ionna set up her light box in the living room.

The thin box had a smooth flat surface and was back lit so she could trace her designs on to fabric. Ionna began by cutting a piece of white cotton fabric and putting it in an embroidery hoop. She placed the pattern she'd drawn for the bluebells on the light box, put the hoop on top, and traced the pattern lightly on to the fabric.

Selecting two shades of blue embroidery thread for the flowers, Ionna began the stitching, using satin stitches for the flower heads and stem stitches for the stems.

Effy cut the pattern pieces for a classic wrap dress. The fabric was a floral print with little bumblebees in the design. It was in her fabric stash, and Ionna loved it. Her sewing machine was set on a table in a corner of the living room, allowing them both plenty of space to work.

There were moments when Ionna was reminded of the past as Effy's sewing machine whirred in the background while she worked on her embroidery designs.

They chatted about crafting, the village, Edinburgh, the publishers, and Effie's website, exchanging news and views of everything.

The morning whizzed by, and they'd both made huge progress with their tasks.

Effy cut the threads from the seam she'd machined, shook the dress and held it up. 'It's shaping up nicely. The fabric is perfect for this style of dress.'

'That was fast work.'

Effy made light of her efficiency and skill, honed from decades of experience. 'I'll rustle us up some lunch. I put the jelly in the fridge to set overnight.' She'd added tinned peaches to the raspberry jelly.

'Do you want me to make the custard?' Ionna offered.

'No, you get on with your embroidery. I'll make the custard and whip up the cream.' Effy went over and peered at Ionna's work. 'The bluebells are beautiful. Your satin stitches on the petals are so smooth.'

'It's been a great morning's work. I'll embroider the pink bluebells after lunch. I always stitch the patterns to see that they work, and make adjustments before sending the artwork away. Though I think these bluebells will work without any changes.' Ionna's experience came to the fore and she'd included bluebells in her previous books, but these were a different design.

Ionna listened to the homely sounds of Effy cooking in the kitchen, lentil soup being heated, bread cut, and the trifle having custard and whipped cream added.

Easing off the tension from her shoulders, Ionna went through to the kitchen when lunch was nearly ready and helped to set up the bowls and plates on the table, and make the tea.

'I'll get you to try on the dress after lunch,' said Effy. 'Wrap dresses are easy to make and they don't need a tailored fit as you can adjust them to suit yourself. I've made a few of these over the years and they're comfy but pretty. Ideal for the summer. And I even wear them in the winter with warm tights and a cardigan. The dress should serve you well when you go back to Edinburgh. The cotton fabric washes up a treat. You'll get a lot of wear out of this dress.'

'Thank you, Effy.'

'Unless you decide to stay in the village a bit longer. Maybe into the autumn. The autumns here are lovely as you know, like an extended summer.'

'I really was only planning to stay for the summer, but I promise I'll think about it.'

'Fair enough, but would it be so difficult to live here instead of Edinburgh? Seeing you work on your designs, it seems to me as if you could create your patterns from anywhere.'

'I'm beginning to wonder that myself. But the city is buzzing with business and it's easy to travel from there. Though I suppose I could travel from the Highlands to London or wherever else was needed for meetings with my publisher and for the book promotions.'

'Something to consider.'

'Yes.'

Effy cleared the soup bowls away. 'Trifle?'

'Oh, yes.'

Effy scooped two portions into pudding bowls and put the remainder in the fridge for later.

They chatted as they enjoyed their trifle.

'The ceilidh should be a laugh tomorrow night,' said Effy.

'I hope I remember the dances.'

'Och, nonsense. You've been ceilidh dancing since you were a wee girl.'

'Do they still include the fast–moving reels?'

'Yes, so wear comfy shoes.'

Ionna's heart felt a surge of excitement, looking forward to the fun night.

'Brochan plays great music, a mix of traditional and modern songs. And there's plenty of room now that they've extended the function area. They serve cocktails in the bar now too. They have a cocktail menu. I've taken a liking to their sherry cocktail. It's one of Brochan's own mixes.'

'I could be tempted to try a cocktail, though I'm not one for drinking. I don't want to overindulge and end up dancing on a table.'

'Forget I mentioned the cocktails. Stick to lemonade. I don't want to encourage you to cause trouble.'

They laughed and continued to eat their trifle.

'I'd like to include a pattern for a cottage in my book,' said Ionna. 'I was wondering if I could embroider your cottage.'

'Embroider my cottage?' Effy sounded surprised.

'Yes, the flowers in the front garden are so pretty — cornflowers, pansies, sunflowers, roses and other flowers. I'd add wee bees buzzing around the lavender at the side of the cottage.'

'I'd love that. To have my cottage as a pattern in your book would be great!'

'It would be a stylised version. I'd use lots of summer blues, pinks, lilac and yellow colours. I picture that I'd satin stitch the roof with crewel wool to give it texture. And I'd make it a sky blue tone.'

'It all sounds great.'

'I'll make a start on the sketch later today.' Ionna was pleased that Effy was happy for the cottage to be part of the book.

'Will it be a secret, or can I tell Jinnet, Mairead and the others?'

'It's not a secret. Tell anyone you want.'

After lunch, Ionna went outside to take photos of the cottage while the sun was shining. The garden was refreshed from the previous night's rain, but had dried in the morning light and everything looked bright and colourful. She took several full view pictures of the cottage and garden, then close–ups of the flowers. Bees buzzed around the lavender and she captured them flying about.

The window frames of the cottage were painted light blue, and the door frame was a slightly deeper tone. The roof was blue–grey, but Ionna planned to emphasise the blue hue making it feel like a summery blue sky.

The scent of the roses mixed with the lavender was a heady fragrance she wished she could bottle and wear whenever she needed a perfume that would remind her of home.

CHAPTER TEN

'Yes, I'm so excited that my cottage is going to be a pattern in Ionna's new embroidery book,' Effy told Jinnet, making a call to the wee shop to tell her the news.

'That will be wonderful. We'll all embroider your cottage when the book comes out,' said Jinnet.

'I'll frame mine and put it up on the living room wall.' Effy sounded happy.

Ionna overheard the conversation as she came in from the garden after taking the photos of the cottage.

'I have to go,' Effy said to Jinnet.

Ionna set up her laptop and transferred the photos. Then she enlarged the images and began sketching the design on paper, glancing at the screen for details.

'I've blabbed to everyone,' Effy said with a giggle, and sat down at her sewing machine to continue making the dress.

Ionna had created cottage patterns for her books before and they'd been popular, so it didn't take her long to sketch the pattern.

She showed the sketch to Effy for approval.

'It's even nicer than I imagined. I'm fair excited.'

Flicking the light box on, Ionna put a piece of white cotton into an embroidery hoop and traced the design on to the fabric.

Then she started the embroidery by stitching the outline of the two side walls in pale grey thread using stem stitch. The white fabric created the look of the whitewashed cottage, and once the window frames were satin stitched light blue, and the door frame outlined with a deeper blue, the cottage started to take shape. Ionna's years of experience had made her a fast worker, and soon she was ready to embroider the roof with blue crewel wool.

'I love the texture the crewel wool gives to the embroidery,' said Ionna, using satin stitches to create the roof.

After finishing the cottage, Ionna embroidered the flowers. She began with the lavender, embroidering the stems and then adding small straight stitches in a lilac tone. The tiny bees were made from straight stitches in chocolate brown and two yellow couching stitches.

The pink, yellow and blue flowers were then embroidered with a combination of lazy daisy stitches, satin stitch and French knots. The greenery was two shades of green in stem stitch.

During the afternoon, Effy stopped to make them a cup of tea, and the chatter circled around the topics they'd been discussing earlier. Now the amber glow of the fading sun created a burnished close to the day.

'This feels like it's been a snow day, without the snow,' Ionna said, working on the last few pieces of the cottage embroidery.

'A coorie in day,' said Effy.

'I like that idea. A coorie in craft day.'

Effy stood up and showed Ionna the wrap dress she'd finished making. 'I'll get you to try it on later.'

'I could put it on now.'

'No, keep going with the cottage embroidery. I'm eager to see it when you've finished it.' Effy checked the time, turned her sewing machine off and tidied away the scraps of fabric and thread she'd used for the dressmaking. 'I'll start making our dinner. Are you going out tonight?'

'No, I'm planning a coorie night in.' Ionna kept sewing, hoping to finish the embroidery before dinner.

Effy went through to the kitchen. 'As we're not going out, I'll make us breaded fish and roast tatties.'

'That sounds delicious.'

'With broccoli and carrots.'

'Are you sure I can't give you a hand with the cooking?'

Effy peered through from the kitchen. 'No, continue with your embroidery.'

Ionna added more details to the flowers, picturing how pretty the cottage pattern would look in the book.

The delicious aroma of dinner cooking wafted through to Ionna. She'd finished the cottage embroidery and tidied some of her things away in her sewing box, but rightly assumed she'd have a coorie craft night after their dinner.

Effy had set the kitchen table and everything was ready.

Ionna washed her hands and helped make the tea while Effy served up the tasty fish, roast tatties and vegetables with slices of lemon, black pepper, and a selection of sauces and relishes.

Scooping up a spoonful of tartar sauce, Ionna added that to her plate along with a couple of pickled onions. 'You're spoiling us this evening, Effy.'

Effy sat down and selected a spicy tomato relish to go with her food. 'This is the first night we've been in relaxing since you arrived. And we'll be out tomorrow night at the ceilidh.'

Ionna cut into the perfectly cooked crisp coating on the fish. 'I'll treat us to dinner at the hub tomorrow before the dancing.'

Effy lifted up her cup of tea. 'You're on. Cheers.'

'Cheers.' Ionna tipped her tea against Effy's cup, and then they tucked into their dinner.

When they finished, Ionna washed the dishes. Both of them were full after having their main course and kept the trifle for later.

'What do you usually do here in the evenings when you're not holding an embroidery bee?' Ionna said, drying the plates and putting them away in the cupboard.

'Embroider, quilt or knit while I watch something on the telly. I'm following up on a thriller series at the moment. There are six episodes and I'm up to episode three.'

'Do you want to watch episode four?' Ionna suggested. 'I'll watch while continuing my embroidery.'

Effy had a better suggestion. 'Let's watch the first episode while we work on our embroidery. I've something that needs finished for a customer. Flowers in a hoop to hang up on their wall.'

'Are you sure? You've seen episode one.'

'It's a watch again series for me. Come on, bring your tea through, and I'll set up the telly.'

Settling down with their respective embroidery, and freshly topped up tea, they sat sewing and watching the show by the glow of two cosy lamps.

Three episodes in, and having scoffed the remainder of the trifle between them for supper, the closing credits rolled on the screen.

'It's a gripping series,' said Ionna, realising she'd finished the cornflower pattern she'd been embroidering. And made a start on a rose design.

'We're a pair of scallywags. I only intended watching the first episode, but I suppose you've caught up with me now.'

'You know what that means,' said Ionna.

'No, what?'

'We can both watch episode four, then call it a night.'

Giggling, Effy pressed play, and they settled down to embroider and watch the show.

'Don't look at the time,' Ionna advised Effy. 'That's what I do when I'm in Edinburgh. I often work late into the night. Then I just tidy up and go to bed.'

Effy took Ionna's advice, and they both tidied their embroidery away, cleaned their cups and got ready for bed.

'I had a great coorie in day and evening,' said Ionna.

'So did I, but we'd better get some sleep so we're fit for the ceilidh dancing. And thank you again for embroidering my cottage. It's gorgeous.'

Heading through to their rooms, the lights in the cottage finally went out.

Tension and thinking about a certain troublemaker had disturbed the early night Leith had planned.

Unable to settle, he'd thrown the covers back, put on his trunks, and gone for a late night swim in the sea.

Swimming along the coast, he'd used his cottage light as the usual beacon, but another marker had kept him on course as he swam further along the shore. The lights from Effy's cottage had been aglow, even at this late hour.

But as he finally waded out of the sea, he noticed the lights were now out.

He surmised that Ionna had gone to bed after working late, or causing some sort of mischief. The lights in Effy's living room had been all aglow, and now the cottage was in darkness.

Leith felt tired enough after his swim to settle himself knowing that Ionna was settled too.

Picking up his towel from the sand, he dried himself roughly, and walked back up to his cottage to shower and get some sleep. He'd worked hard all day on the cottages, and into the early evening. Huge progress had been made on the renovations. Huge backward moves regarding his feelings for Ionna.

Chiding himself for some of the harsh things he'd said to her the previous night, he washed the sea water from his body and then dried off and went to bed.

The kitchen door was open, letting the fresh summer air and the scent of the flowers in the back garden waft in as Effy cooked the porridge for their breakfast.

Ionna walked through wearing the new dress Effy had made and gave her a twirl.

'Oh, it suits you.'

Ionna ran her hands down the floral print fabric that had little bumblebees in the design. 'I match the cottage. Pretty flowers and bumbles.'

They sat down to breakfast and discussed their plans for the day.

'I noticed the parcels on the hall table ready for posting. Do you want me to drop them off at the wee shop?' Ionna offered. 'I'd like to have a donner down to the main street this morning.'

'If you wouldn't mind. I have an account with Jinnet. You just need to hand the parcels over to her.'

'I can do that. And it'll give my new dress it's first outing.'

'It's going to be a warm sunny day. There's heat in the sun already. I was out the back door getting a boost of fresh air to wake me up after our late night. But I feel none the worse for it.'

'I'm a bad influence on you.'

'Aye, you always were.'

A knock on the front door interrupted their conversation.

'I'm not expecting anyone this early,' said Effy, hurrying through to the hall.

Ionna heard the familiar voice of Mairead, and Effy inviting her in.

'I hope I'm not disturbing your breakfast,' said Mairead.

'Not at all,' Effy assured her, bringing her into the living room.

Ionna peeked through and smiled. 'Morning, Mairead.'

'I finished your shift dress.' Mairead held up her craft bag.

Ionna jumped up excitedly and went to take a look.

Mairead lifted it carefully out of the bag. She'd ironed and folded it. 'Do you want to try it on? It'll let me know if it needs any alterations.'

Thrilled with the dress, Ionna went through to her bedroom, put it on and came hurrying back through to the living room. The wide smile on her face told Mairead that she was happy with the design. The cotton mix fabric was a subtle print of blues and neutral tones including light grey.'

'I added two pockets to the front of the skirt,' said Mairead. 'I find them so handy.'

'They are.' Ionna dug her hands into the deep pockets that were both practical for holding her phone and other items instead of carrying a bag, and added to the design of the shift dress.

'The colours are easy to mix and match with a short sleeve top for mild days, though it's a scorcher this morning so it's ideal to wear on its own,' said Mairead. 'And worn with a long sleeve top or jumper it's adaptable for the winter.'

Ionna gave Mairead a hug. 'I appreciate all the work you've put into this.'

'Och, these dresses are an easy pattern and stitch up a treat,' said Mairead.

'The dress I had on this morning is one that Effy made for me,' said Ionna. 'I'm being spoiled rotten.'

'Would you like a cup of tea?' Effy offered Mairead. 'There's plenty in the pot.'

'Yes, thanks.' Mairead followed Effy into the kitchen.

Ionna kept the shift dress on and put the parcels in a quilted tote bag. 'I'll pop down and post these, Effy. Do you need anything from the shop while I'm there?'

'A fresh loaf,' said Effy, pouring a cup of tea for Mairead and getting ready for a natter.

'I'll pick that up,' Ionna promised and headed out into the sunshine.

The cottage had a beautiful sea view and Ionna admired the coastal scenery as she walked to the nearby main street.

She saw the wee shop looking pretty in the sunlight, and walked in to find Jinnet stocking up the fresh vegetables in her window display.

'I like your shift dress,' Jinnet said with a welcoming smile.

'Mairead made it for me. It feels great to wear.' She put the parcels on the counter. 'Effy said you deal with her parcels.'

'Yes, the courier arrives later today. I'll get these sent off.'

Ionna picked up a loaf and one of the cauliflowers on display. Jinnet rang the items through the till and put the cauliflower in a paper bag.

'Are you and Effy still going to the ceilidh tonight?' said Jinnet.

'Yes, and we're having dinner in the hub before it starts.'

'The new menu is delicious.'

'Anything you'd recommend?' said Ionna.

'Everything.'

Laughing, Ionna put her groceries in the tote bag. 'I'll see you later, Jinnet.'

Ionna was so busy thinking that she'd wear the new wrap dress Effy had made for her to the ceilidh instead of the white broderie anglaise, that she didn't take in the tall figure working on one of the cottages nearby.

Walking past the cottage's extensive front garden, she saw the most perfect Cupid's dart flowers. And stopped. The blue flowers were gorgeous and she dug her phone from the pocket of her dress and took a picture. Checking the image, she wished she could get a close–up of the fabulous blue petals and the long grey–green stems. She hadn't seen these flowers for years. Not since she'd left the village. And Effy didn't have them in her garden. But here they were, just over the low hedging.

Leith had stepped back out of the sunlight and was watching her antics from the shade of the garden tree. She looked pretty in her dress, and mischievous. He knew that look.

Attempting to lean over without stepping into the garden, Ionna put her bag down and overstretched to take a picture of the flowers.

'You're welcome to use the gate and come in,' he called over to her.

The sound of Leith's voice jarred her, and as she glanced at the figure shaded by the tree, and tried not to topple into the garden as she overreached, she tumbled head–over–heels across the hedge.

136

Leith ran over, trying to catch her from falling, but she'd flipped so fast and in spectacular fashion that he could barely contain his laughter.

Jumping up from her ungainly stumble, Ionna shook her blonde hair back from her face and tried not to look embarrassed.

'Laugh and get it over with,' she said, giving him a challenging stare.

Leith smirked at her. 'I'm going to give you the benefit of the doubt and assume you took gymnastic lessons in the city, and you're just keeping your hand in, because that was an impressive tumble the cran.'

Flustered, she tugged down the hem of her dress, hoping he hadn't seen her knickers.

'I didn't see your blue unmentionables,' he lied, still smirking.

In no mood to trade barbed remarks with him, she picked up her bag and marched away.

He watched her for a moment and then called after her. 'I'm sorry, Ionna!'

She pretended that the sea breeze had blown away his apology, but he could tell from the flick of her hair and straightening of her shoulders that she'd heard him.

Mairead had left by the time Ionna got back to Effy's cottage, still bristling from her embarrassing encounter with Leith.

Effy was in the kitchen. 'Did you get the parcels posted?'

'Yes, and I got fresh bread and a cauliflower.' Ionna unpacked them from the bag and put them on the kitchen table.

'Are you okay?' Effy sensed she was tense and annoyed.

Ionna told her what happened with Leith.

'Don't upset yourself,' said Effy.

Smiling tightly, Ionna went through to the living room and started to work on her embroidery designs, hoping that concentrating on the patterns would ease her annoyance.

She sat at the table near the window, sketching and figuring out the patterns for the roses. The sunlight streamed in, and she started to calm down.

Leith continued his building work, and as he went to his van that was parked outside the garden, he noticed Ionna's phone lying on the grass. As he picked it up a call came through and he saw the caller's name — *publishers*.

Concerned that Ionna would miss an important call from her publishers, he answered it.

'Hello,' he said.

A moment's hesitation and then a woman's polite voice came through. 'Is Ionna there?'

'She's not here at the moment. I have her phone. But I'm heading to her cottage right now.'

'Is that Matt?' The woman sounded curious. 'Are you Ionna's boyfriend?'

'No, I'm Leith. I'm Ionna's...' What? Friend? Annoying acquaintance?

Before he could think of his appropriate label, the woman spoke up. 'Could you get Ionna to call me. Tell her it's Lucy, her editor.'

'Okay, Lucy, I'll do that.'

'Thanks, Leith. Bye.'

'Was Leith wearing his clothes?' Effy said, trying to lighten the mood as she brought Ionna a cup of tea.

'He was fully clothed, and wearing a smirk.' Ionna sounded less upset.

Leaving Ionna to have her tea and work on her embroidery, Effy went out to the back garden to hang a few items to dry on her washing line.

Leith walked up to Effy's cottage and saw her in the back garden.

Effy looked surprised to see him as she hung up the clean dish towels.

'Ionna dropped her phone. It fell on the grass so it's not damaged.' He held it up. 'Her publishers just phoned. Lucy wants Ionna to call her back.' He explained why he'd taken the call.

Effy accepted the phone and his reason for answering it.

'I'll tell her. She's busy with her embroidery in the living room.'

Leith went to walk away, sensing Effy was less than happy with him. Then he spoke up. 'I tried to apologise to Ionna. I seem to keep saying the wrong things.'

'Maybe you could try being more of a gentleman the next time. You should've checked to see if she'd hurt herself from the tumble. Instead you embarrassed her with a jibe about her knickers.'

Leith took the telling off, agreeing with Effy. 'Tell Ionna I'm sorry.'

'She heard you.'

He sighed heavily. 'I'll try to be more of a gentleman.'

Effy looked him up and down. 'At least you're wearing all your clothes. That's an improvement.'

He almost smiled as he walked away.

Effy hurried inside. 'Leith found your phone. You'd dropped it when you tumbled. He took a call from your publishers.'

'He what?' Ionna exclaimed.

'Lucy wants you to phone her. Do that first, and then I'll tell you what Leith said.'

Ionna made the call to her editor.

Effy busied herself in the kitchen, preparing the large cauliflower and putting it in a pot of water to boil, but she could overhear the gist of the conversation.

'I've already designed several new patterns,' Ionna told Lucy, giving her an update on the book. 'I'll email you the sketches and some of the inked artwork, and photos of a few of the embroideries I've stitched since I arrived.'

'That was fast work.' Lucy sounded impressed.

'There are so many beautiful flowers here. The laird invited me up to the castle's rose garden, and I'll design various rose patterns. The castle's forest has bluebells, and I've embroidered the blue version, but there were pink bluebells too.'

'Pink bluebells? They sound great,' said Lucy.

'And other flowers I'm working on are pansies, freesia, sunflowers, jasmine, cornflowers and thistles. The thistles will be a mix of embroidery thread and crewel wool. And I took pictures of gorgeous blue Cupid's dart flowers this morning. I'll sketch some designs for them soon.'

'Well, you seem to be making great headway with the book,' Lucy told her.

'I have, and I've designed a cottage pattern, based on my Aunt Effy's cottage and garden. I satin stitched the roof with crewel wool, but everything else is embroidered with thread. I've finished embroidering it, so I'll send you pictures, and once you approve the designs, I'll post the actual embroideries to you so you can have them photographed for the book.'

'Perfect,' said Lucy. 'Email me whatever you have. We'll speak soon. Wonderful work, Ionna.'

Ionna smiled as the call finished on a happy note, and she went through to talk to Effy.

'I'm going to email the patterns and pictures off to the publishers right now. But I'd like to hear what Leith said.'

'He's got a real bee in his bonnet about you. But I sent him off with a flea in his ear.' Effy told her what happened as Ionna set up the information on her laptop in the living room to send to her editor.

'Did he take the telling off?'

'He did. Leith says he's going to try to be more of a gentleman.'

Ionna scoffed.

After sending the information away, Ionna went through to the kitchen.

'I thought I'd make us cauliflower cheese for our lunch,' said Effy, taking out the Scottish cheddar from the fridge. 'Thanks for buying it. This will be a light and tasty lunch so we're ready for our dinner at the hub.'

'I've decided to wear the wrap dress you made for me.'

Effy was delighted.

'Do you think Leith will turn up at the ceilidh?' said Ionna.

'Maybe, but Leith doesn't go to the ceilidh nights often. And the laird never turns up. But there will be plenty of other men to dance with.'

Ionna smiled, looking forward to a night of ceilidh dancing.

CHAPTER ELEVEN

The evening air was warm as Ionna and Effy walked along to the hub for dinner. Lights shone from the windows of the bar restaurant and cast a welcoming glow on to the main street where it was situated in the heart of the village with a view of the sea.

Ionna wore her new dress. Effy opted for a tea dress and a cardigan.

The hub was pleasantly busy when they went inside. Music played in the background and blended with the chatter of people sitting having dinner at the tables in the restaurant area and at the bar. Mirrors along the full length of the bar reflected the large selection of drinks. Bottles of whisky, brandy, rum and cognac matched the warm decor of deep burgundy and cream with shiny gold balustrades. Chestnut tone wooden chairs and tables blended with the polished wood flooring that extended through to the function room.

Bhictoria was the first to welcome Ionna and Effy and waved them over to the bar.

'We're here for our dinner,' said Ionna. 'If there's a table available.'

'There is. I'll get you seated in a minute.' Bhictoria wore a tartan–trimmed dress and her dark auburn hair was pinned up in a bun. She called over to Brochan. He had his kilt on and was busy mixing cocktails. 'Ionna and Effy are here.'

Brochan glanced round and his face lit up with a smile. He put the bottles of whisky and liqueurs down and hurried over. Tall and sturdy, with a flurry of light auburn hair, he suited the kilt he was wearing. 'It's great to see you, Ionna. Can I make you a welcome home cocktail? And a sherry cocktail for you, Effy.'

'Yes, but not too strong,' said Ionna.

'I'll make you a light fruity one with plenty of fizz,' he said, setting up the glasses and deftly picking up the bottles he needed for the cocktails.

'They're in for dinner,' Bhictoria told him, leading them away to a table and handing them the menus.

'Jinnet was right,' said Ionna, glancing at her menu. 'Everything looks delicious.'

'I can recommend Brochan's savoury lattice pie,' said Bhictoria. Brochan was an excellent chef and cooked many of the dishes, and they had kitchen and waiting staff to assist with the running of the hub. Bhictoria helped with the cooking too, and her soups were popular.

Ionna and Effy opted for the lattice pie that had light puff pastry and was served with mashed tatties, broccoli, carrots and peas.

As Bhictoria hurried away through to the kitchen to get their order, Brochan came over carrying their cocktails.

'Here you go, girls, cocktails on the house as a welcome home to Ionna,' he said, presenting their drinks. Effy's sherry cocktail was served in a tall glass with a twist of lemon and a cherry. Ionna's cocktail looked like raspberry lemonade garnished with fresh fruit including slices of orange and lime.

'Thank you, Brochan,' said Ionna.

Effy lifted up her sherry cocktail. 'Cheers,' she said to him.

Brochan bounded away back to the bar as Bhictoria arrived with their main course.

'This looks delicious,' Ionna enthused. 'The puff pastry is light as air.'

'Brochan's renowned for his well–risen pastry,' said Bhictoria. 'My husband has always been able to rise to the occasion in the kitchen.' Smiling, she let them enjoy their dinner while she went away to serve other customers.

'This pie really is delicious,' said Ionna, cutting into the pastry. Then she looked around. 'Most of the men are wearing their kilts.'

'The ceilidh nights are popular,' said Effy, enjoying her dinner.

A poster on the wall advertised the various activities that were scheduled in the evenings at the hub, including dominoes.

Ionna read the poster. 'There's something on nearly every night. Party events, fancy dress, theme nights.'

'The hub nights are fun.' Effy checked the poster. 'We should go to a few while you're here.'

'Okay.'

From where she was sitting, Ionna could see through to the extended function room. The lights were on and a few people were seated at the small tables around the dance floor.

'The new extension certainly has a bigger dance floor,' Ionna commented.

'It's great for the ceilidh dancing.'

Ionna thought about Leith being the architect and the main builder. 'Does Leith do a lot of the local building work?'

'Yes, he does well for himself,' said Effy, finishing her dinner. 'He does most of the building work in the village and he works in the nearby towns.'

They continued to chat and checked the menu for pudding.

'I know what I'll have,' said Ionna. 'Cranachan. It's my favourite. I love the fresh raspberries and double cream.'

'I'll have the ice cream special with chocolate sauce.'

They ordered their puddings.

Ionna's was served up in a glass and had layers of fresh raspberries, honey, oatmeal and cream. She scooped up a mouthful and nodded.

Effy was about to dig her spoon into the meringue and chocolate topping of her ice cream when she saw some of the crafting bee ladies arrive. Mairead, Vaila, Jinnet and Ailish waved over to them as they headed through to the function room. They were all wearing dresses for the dancing.

'The ladies always arrive early so they can settle in their seats,' Effy told Ionna. 'We've plenty of time to enjoy our meal before the ceilidh starts.'

Donal and Gorden arrived wearing their kilts and went up to get a drink at the bar, both nodding acknowledgement over to Ionna and Effy.

'Roary will be on his own tonight up at the castle,' Ionna commented.

'He always is,' said Effy. 'The staff don't stay at the castle. Once they finish their work for the day, they leave. Gorden's usually the last to leave after he serves the laird his dinner.'

Ionna pictured Roary sitting in his living room reading a book or playing chess. 'It's a big castle to rattle around in on your own. I wouldn't fancy that.'

'The castle has always been his home. Apart from staying in hotel rooms on his business trips, it's all he's ever known. If he gets married and has a family of his own one day, that'll liven it up.'

'Or be more sociable with local folk,' said Ionna. 'Hold more parties and dances at the castle.'

Ionna ate her cranachan and continued chatting to Effy as the hub started to become busier.

Brochan went swaggering past in his kilt and headed through to the function room to sort out the music for the ceilidh. He had a great selection of traditional and popular songs that suited the various dances. The quiet background music in the hub soon became a lively number as he geared up to get the ceilidh started. He altered the list of music and dances for every party so that it kept things lively. No two ceilidh nights were the same, encouraging people to attend on a regular basis. And since they'd extended the dance floor, this had added to the popularity of the ceilidhs.

After setting up the music, Brochan hurried through to the bar.

Bhictoria opened the cloakroom door in the back of the function room and the crafting bee ladies hung their bags and jackets in there and chatted excitedly about the ceilidh dancing.

'Brochan is planning to kick things off with a lively reel,' Bhictoria told the ladies. 'There's an added excitement to the atmosphere this evening. I think we're in for a rousing night.'

'We noticed Effy and Ionna through in the restaurant having their dinner,' said Jinnet.

'Yes, Ionna's treating Effy to dinner, but they'll be through to join in the dancing once it starts,' Bhictoria assured them. 'Away and grab your seats. I'll get you a round of your usual drinks.'

Bustling and chatting with excitement, the ladies went to their seats while Bhictoria headed through to the bar.

'There you go, hen.' Brochan smiled at Bhictoria, handing her a tray with the four cocktails for the ladies. No two were the same. Mairead's was malt whisky based, Vaila liked a cognac cocktail, Jinnet's taste was light and fruity, and Ailish's concoction looked quite tropical.

'You're way ahead of me,' Bhictoria said with a smile, and carried the drinks through to the function room.

Jinnet craned her neck to see through to the front of the hub.

'Peeking at Gorden?' Mairead teased Jinnet.

'No, and there's nothing going us between us,' Jinnet insisted. 'I'm happy with my wee shop and my crafts.'

Smirks from the ladies made her laugh.

'I bet Gorden makes a beeline for you, Jinnet, when the dancing starts,' said Mairead.

'Gorden's been quite friendly this past wee while,' Jinnet admitted. 'I'll have a dance with him, but that's all. I was actually looking to see if Leith had arrived. When he was in my shop, he said that he might give his kilt an airing.'

'Do you think the laird will turn up now that Ionna is here?' said Vaila.

Bhictoria put the tray of drinks down on the table, cutting–in when she heard the topic of their conversation. 'Brochan was chatting to Donal and Gorden. They said that when they left the castle the laird was settled down for the night reading a book in his living room.'

'That man needs to get out and socialise more,' said Ailish.

'According to Donal, the laird parties plenty when he's on his business trips,' Bhictoria explained. 'Apparently, he looks forward to relaxing when he gets home to the castle.'

'Roary is an expert ceilidh dancer,' Vaila remarked. 'Remember how high he could leap when he was doing the Highland Fling at the castle's New Year ball?'

They did.

'I didn't know where to look,' said Ailish, causing the others to giggle.

'Oops! Brochan's waving at me,' Bhictoria said, noticing him behind the increasingly busy bar. 'I'd better go and help with the orders.'

The four ladies lifted up their glasses to Bhictoria. 'See you on the dance floor!'

Laughing, Bhictoria hurried away. As hosts of the hub, Brochan and Bhictoria joined in a lot of the dances.

Leith stood in front of the wardrobe mirror and started taking items of his kilted attire off. The night was warm, and that surely meant that the hub would be hoachin' with revellers and his full–kilted outfit would be too hot.

The black kilt jacket with its shiny buttons came off first, then the black waistcoat that was buttoned up over his white shirt and tie. Did he really need a sporran, he wondered. Yes, it was handy for keeping his wallet safe.

Buckling the sporran, he tucked his wallet inside, then assessed what was left. The knee–length wool socks and brogues. Those were fine. As was the kilt itself, in shades of dark turquoise tartan that reminded him of the colours of the evening sea.

He stepped back for a full view. To wear a tie or not? Off came the tie. As he stripped down to his kilt and open neck shirt, he smiled to himself thinking that he was the cause of casting aside his clothes this time, not Ionna.

His freshly showered hair had an auburn gold, sun–lightened wave rising up from his brow. But there was doubt in his eyes whether he should forgo a night at the ceilidh, knowing that Ionna would be attending. Then again, she'd promised him a dance. That rare pleasure was worth risking a night full of mischief and trouble.

Adding his keys to his sporran, Leith strode away from his cottage and walked to the hub in the main street. From a distance, he could see the lights were ablaze, and the activity as folk arrived to join in the fun.

The atmosphere washed over him as he stepped inside. Using his tall stature to peer over the numerous heads at the bar, he nodded acknowledgement to Brochan busy pouring drinks. Bhictoria's eyes widened along with her smile when she saw Leith, the infrequent ceilidh customer.

With his focus on heading through to the function room, hearing the music, but no sign that the dancing had started, Leith didn't notice Ionna and Effy sitting in the restaurant sipping their cocktails.

But they noticed him.

'Leith's here!' Effy whispered urgently.

Ionna's heart jolted unexpectedly, feeling a surge of excitement that he'd arrived.

'I promised him a dance.'

'Seeing how handsome he's looking all dressed up in his kilt, I think he's here to collect,' said Effy.

Night is never as dark as you think it will be.

This sentiment was instilled in Roary when he was a wee boy by his father the former laird. When they'd walk at night from the castle through the forest and down to the sea, Roary had learned not to fret about walking there at night.

Shadows and light created an atmosphere of adventure. And anything hiding in the gloaming, lurking in the dark, would soon realise their mistake. They were the prey if they tackled him, not Roary.

But in all the years of living at the castle in the forest, he'd never encountered anything or anyone that challenged him, other than downpours of rain from unexpected storms. And even then, Roary knew where there were thick overarching trees providing a canopy for shelter. Though more often, his father's other phrase — *You won't melt* — served him well when he had to walk in the rain, and he'd venture on to wherever he'd intended heading.

Dressed in his kilted finery — a kilt in dark green tones, sporran, thick socks with tartan flashes tucked into the folds, brogues, the white ghillie shirt he'd worn for the magazine shoot, likewise, the dark jacket and waistcoat. The top laces of the shirt were undone. Everything else was buttoned tight.

Roary's resolve to attend the ceilidh didn't falter as he made his way through the heart of the forest. His soft as butter brogues had soles for dancing, but helped him navigate the gnarled tree roots.

The sliver of a silvery moon shone through the branches overhead and patches of sky where the trees didn't overarch sparkled with stars.

It was a fine night for a venture through the forest, and he could feel the atmosphere invigorate him, along with the anticipation of dancing with Ionna.

CHAPTER TWELVE

The remainder of the crafting bee ladies had arrived at the hub and were all sitting together in the function room. They'd kept two seats for Ionna and Effy.

Brochan stood behind the DJ–style set up that he had on the small stage, lining up the music for the dances. The room was busy with people anticipating the first dance of the evening.

When Ionna and Effy came through from the restaurant they put their bags in the cloakroom and then sat down between Jinnet and Ailish. Remnants of the cocktails were in the glasses they put on the table.

One of the farmers had waylaid Leith, praising him for the recent building work he'd done on the farmhouse. Leith didn't see Ionna and Effy go by, though they noticed him. It was difficult to miss his tall stature even among the strapping farmers, crofters and other local men. His auburn hair shone like burnished gold under the lights that illuminated the function room. He'd installed them himself.

Ionna's heart started racing and she told herself to calm down. Whatever had gotten into her? It was Leith. Yes, he was a handsome man, but...

'Ionna has designed a beautiful embroidery pattern of my cottage.' Effy discussed the pattern with the ladies.

Ionna blinked out of her wayward thoughts.

'She's embroidered the roof with crewel wool to create a soft texture', Effy continued. 'The blue colour tones in with the window frames and the door.'

The interest shown in this merited further discussion, and giving the ladies her full attention rather than watching Leith, Ionna showed them pictures on her phone of the finished embroidery.

Amid further discussion about the pattern, how many strands of embroidery thread she'd used for the lazy daisy stitches on the flowers, her tiny bees buzzing around the lavender, Leith made his way over to the ladies.

Brochan was gearing up to announce the start of the ceilidh, and folk were already partnering up.

Leith's heart pounded as he approached. Ionna had promised him a dance, but if he collected it right now, would it cause the gossip to spark around her? Would it be better to forgo the promise? Decision made, he walked up to the ladies.

'Good evening,' he said politely.

All the ladies expected him to then invite Ionna to join him in the first dance that was about to start.

Instead, Leith spoke to Ailish. 'I don't want to take up your time this evening with business. But I wondered if I could discuss the fabric for the items I need for the cottages. Not tonight, but soon.'

Ailish was as surprised as the other ladies that he wanted to discuss fabric and not immediately flirt with Ionna. 'Yes, I've put fabric aside for you that matches the swatches I gave you. Drop by the cottage tomorrow if it's convenient and we'll finalise the fabric for the curtains, cushions and quilts.'

'I'll come round mid–morning, if that's suitable,' said Leith. This task was pressing, but he hoped to alleviate the gossip.

'That's ideal,' Ailish confirmed.

The music changed as the ceilidh was about to start.

'Would you like to step on to the dance floor folks,' Brochan announced. 'We'll begin the ceilidh with a rousing reel. No partners needed. Everyone up, and form a large circle.'

Ionna was swept away with the ladies as they got up immediately to take their place on the dance floor that was quickly filling up with people eager to join in the reel.

Leith hung back, not planning on taking part in the first reel, but he was pulled in by revellers encouraging him to dance.

Amid the merriment, Leith linked arms during the reel with Effy, Mairead and Jinnet, but didn't come close to dancing with Ionna.

As the music finished he ended up standing next to Ionna and took a moment to tell her something before the next dance began.

'I know you promised me a dance,' Leith said in a confiding tone. 'But I'm not going to hold you to it. I don't want to stir up any further gossip for you.'

'That's very gentlemanly of you,' Ionna said, taken aback.

Leith then stepped away as Brochan announced a jig.

'Take your partners for the first jig of the evening,' said Brochan.

As Leith moved away another man moved in and Ionna danced with him, a crofter she vaguely knew from the past.

Leith pressed his back against the wall and watched as Ionna danced the jig that he would've danced with her. But he'd made the right decision, he told himself, even though he wished she was dancing with him. Watching her on the dance floor, he thought she looked beautiful in her pretty dress.

The social aspects of the ceilidhs in the hub encouraged everyone to dance with everyone else, even though couples tended to stick together most of the time.

A few couples were there, and Leith wondered if one day he'd have that type of happiness.

Pushing away thoughts that only twisted knots in his guts, he let the music and the lively atmosphere drift around him, feeling apart from everyone.

When the jig finished, the man smiled at Ionna and then went back to join his friends.

Effy spoke hurriedly to Ionna as another song's introduction began. 'Why didn't you dance with Leith?' She'd seen him talk to Ionna and then walk away.

'Because he didn't ask me.' Ionna revealed his reason.

Effy looked surprised. 'Maybe he's trying to be a gentleman after all.'

Ionna agreed, and yet her heart wouldn't settle.

Before she could dwell on the issue, the ladies pulled her on to the dance floor where she enjoyed a fast–moving reel, dancing with various people. And then another lively dance.

By now, Leith had joined in and was burling around the floor and holding his arms up with other ladies forming an archway for folk to dance under.

Ionna, partnered with Donal, skip–stepped underneath Leith's arch, and smiled at him as she went by.

One smile warmed Leith's heart more than all the energetic dancing.

Brochan overlapped the music into another reel, keeping the ceilidh going, and everyone stayed on the dance floor including Ionna and Leith.

He'd calculated that in another two rounds of the reel, he'd get to dance for a few moments with Ionna as the sequence circled to change partners.

But something happened in the front bar and restaurant to tilt the atmosphere into a tense mode.

Ionna and others sensed it too, and as they danced they tried to see what it was. Trouble of some sort? She couldn't see over the crowd as people began stare through to the bar.

But Leith could. He saw the reason for the change in the energy.

Roary had arrived.

Bhictoria hid her surprise behind a welcoming smile as the tall, handsome figure of the laird walked into the hub.

'Are you here for the ceilidh?' Bhictoria called over to him.

'I am.' The assuredness of the deep voice rose above the rabble.

People didn't hide their surprise, and whispered to each other, nudging and indicating to those around them that the laird was in their midst. A rare visit from him to the hub.

'Would you like a drink before you go through?' Bhictoria said to Roary, expecting him to refuse, but hoping it would give her time to send a secret alert to Brochan.

Unaware that the laird had arrived, Brochan continued to play the music in the function room.

'I'll have a dram, Bhictoria,' said Roary, walking up to the bar, opening his sporran to get money to pay for it.

'It's on the house,' Bhictoria told him, pouring him one of their finest whiskies, while secretly pressing the call button on her phone.

Brochan had stepped out from behind the music desk to whip up encouragement and instruction to the dancers. In full view of them, his sporran started to jump and jiggle.

'What have you got hidden in your sporran, Brochan?' Donal shouted out jokingly.

Brochan laughed and darted back behind the desk. He reached into his sporran and turned off the alert on his second phone. Used only in cases of hub emergencies. A signal from Bhictoria that something was happening — perhaps a stramash. When the hub was busy and they were working in different parts, unable to hurry through to tell each other, this was their tried and true method of alert.

Bhictoria thought that the laird turning up for the ceilidh merited the signal, especially as she surmised he wasn't there for the dancing, but to woo Ionna. As

Leith was present, rival fireworks between the two men could spark.

Brochan looked around on high alert. Peering over the crowd through to the bar, he saw Bhictoria give him a second signal. Waving a tea towel in a whirly above her head, told him to look at the folk standing around the bar. And that's when he saw the laird picking up the small glass of whisky, downing the dram in one gulp, and then making his way through to the function room.

Nodding firmly to his wife, Brochan kept the music going, continuing the reel with a second song while he made his way through the crowd to greet the laird.

Brochan wasn't fast enough, and Roary had a determination in him as he saw Ionna dancing the reel. Knowing the steps better than most, he timed it perfectly to cut–in and replace her current partner.

Like a nifty slight of hand, she was now dancing with Roary.

Breathless from the fast–moving dances, one after the other, and from the surprise of seeing Roary there in his finery, Ionna wasn't able to hide the effect of his arrival.

Ionna gasped. 'I didn't expect to see you here,' she said as his hands clasped hers and they twirled around on the spot.

'I thought a night of ceilidh dancing would be fun.' He then almost lifted her off the floor with his strength as they danced around.

Effy was sitting this one out, along with Mairead and Jinnet.

'Did you see Roary cut–in to dance with Ionna?' Effy sounded aghast.

'Look at Leith's face,' said Jinnet.

They glanced over at Leith's glum reaction as he watched Ionna dancing with the laird.

'Leith's not happy,' Mairead agreed.

'I hope there's not going to be trouble,' Jinnet added.

'Haud my cocktail.' Effy handed her second sherry cocktail of the evening to Mairead. 'I'm away to warn Brochan.'

Jinnet pulled Effy back. 'Did you not see his sporran jumping? Bhictoria has already alerted him.'

Effy took her cocktail back and downed a gulp. 'Roary never turns up to the ceilidhs. It's clear what's enticed him here tonight.'

Bhictoria's signal with the tea towel gave Brochan an idea. There was a dance that included what he called a whirly, and it had a tendency to clear the dance floor. Some folk liked to watch from the side, while others were keen to team up and try their hand at the fun movement that was part of the dance.

Brochan lined up the song he used for this and then announced the dance with the whirly movement in it. 'So team up. Two lads and two lassies.'

People started to team up, while others stood aside looking forward to watching the fun.

Roary was in clear view now and being admired by several of the ladies.

'Wow! The laird is looking gorgeous in his kilt,' Vaila whispered to Ailish.

'He's certainly making a play for Ionna,' Ailish remarked. 'He's got a hold of her hand.'

'She's the one that flirted with him in the forest,' said Vaila.

Other gossip was circulating around as people partnered up.

Brochan saw that Roary and Ionna hadn't yet found anyone to partner with. The only man remaining was Leith, standing nearby Ailish and Vaila.

Roary wanted to take part, so he looked over at Leith and gave him an encouraging nod.

'Would you like to dance?' Leith said to Ailish.

'No, I'm sitting this one out,' she said.

'I'll do it.' Vaila stepped forward and accompanied Leith over to Roary and Ionna.

Ionna was hesitant, especially as she could sense the tension between Leith and the laird. But as the introduction to the song began, she became part of the foursome.

After skip–stepping as two separate couples, it was time for the whirly movement.

The four of them faced each other in a huddle. The two lads facing opposite each other, and the two lassies facing each other as well. Then Ionna and Vaila put their arms around the shoulders of Roary and Leith, while the men wrapped their strong arms around Ionna and Vaila's backs at waist level. Using their strength and momentum, the men lifted the women up while turning around on the spot. Ionna and Vaila, hanging on tight, lifted their feet off the floor. Their legs were out behind them, in a whirly motion, as the men spun in time to the lively music.

Laughter and cheers filled the function room.

Ionna felt the muscles of Roary and Leith as she gripped on to their shoulders.

Then it was back to the skip–stepping, before repeating the whirly fun. This continued until the end of the dance.

Gorden had invited Jinnet to dance with him, and they'd partnered up with Donal and Effy.

Ionna could hear the squeals of laughter from Effy and Jinnet, and others taking part.

Finally, the dance finished with rousing cheers and applause.

Vaila tried to engage Roary in light chatter, but he politely steered the conversation to Leith.

'Can I have a word with you?' Roary said to him.

'Yes,' Leith replied firmly.

'In private,' said Roary.

With a glance and smile at Ionna and Vaila, the two men excused themselves and went over to the function room's patio doors and stepped outside to talk.

Ionna and the other ladies watched them through the glass doors.

Effy came hurrying over to Ionna. 'What happened? Are they arguing over something?' Effy's expression indicated it was probably over Ionna.

'Roary wanted to talk to Leith in private,' Ionna told Effy.

Another dance started, and one of the farmers invited Vaila to dance with him and she accepted.

Gorden clasped Jinnet's hand and they started to dance together.

Several of the crafting bee ladies were up dancing with farmers, crofters and other local men. And Bhictoria danced with Brochan.

Ionna stood on her own, watching and wondering what Roary and Leith were discussing. Deep in conversation, they didn't appear to be arguing, but their discussion seemed fairly intense. It lasted for the full length of the reel, extended into the next jig, and by this time she'd joined in the dancing rather than stand and watch the pair of them. No doubt, she'd soon find out what they'd discussed. But she was here to enjoy the ceilidh night with Effy and the other ladies, she reminded herself firmly.

Roary and Leith finally came back in.

Ionna was on the dance floor and Roary stood at the side instead of cutting–in, but as soon as the dance finished, he approached her. 'Can I buy you a drink?'

She was going to refuse, then changed her mind. 'Yes, I'll have a cocktail. The same one Brochan made me earlier.'

'I'll be back in a few minutes,' said Roary, making his way through to the bar. It was a novelty having the laird there, and customers made way for him and he was served fairly fast.

Leith didn't look across at Ionna, and she felt her heart react when he went over and spoke to Ailish. After chatting happily for a couple of minutes, they partnered up for a waltz.

'Here you go,' Roary said, handing her the cocktail, while he opted for another dram of whisky.

Ionna clasped the glass and took a sip, while trying not to feel upset seeing Leith waltzing with Ailish. The unfamiliar feeling jarred her.

Roary saw her looking over at them waltzing. He downed his whisky, put the glass on a table and took Ionna's hand. 'Come and waltz with me.'

And she did. They waltzed past Leith and Ailish who were too busy chatting while they danced to notice her.

Roary gazed down at her, and nothing in her heart stirred.

'Are you okay?' Roary said to her.

'Yes, fine.'

Clearly she wasn't fine. Roary pulled her close and they waltzed under the spotlights not saying a word, while she saw Leith and Ailish chatting cheerily.

Ionna felt like she was living the dream she'd had so long ago — dancing a romantic waltz with Roary. Now, she couldn't turn the clock back, and she couldn't force herself to feel the way she used to about him. She was never in the right relationship with the right man at the right time. Her heart's timing when it came to romance was always off–kilter.

Roary was sharp enough to sense that Ionna wasn't interested in him. Despite the flirting in the forest, he knew he was waltzing with a woman who wished she was dancing with someone else. Leith. Rejection was an unfamiliar feeling for the laird. He was so used to women being enamoured with him. So it was all the more evident that she really didn't have a crush on him now.

Should he try to win her heart if somehow she decided to stay in the village rather than go back to Edinburgh? He'd sleep on his decision. The night hadn't gone according to his plans. He needed to redraw them.

Holding Ionna close, they waltzed until the end of the song, then he bid her goodnight.

'Goodnight, Roary,' she murmured, sensing it was more of a goodbye. She'd never said goodbye to him the last time. Maybe it was better this way.

The laird left the hub and disappeared into the night, taking some of the tension with him.

Ailish had finished dancing with Leith and was now chatting to Effy, Mairead and Jinnet.

Leith approached Ionna as another waltz played, a slower number.

'Would you like to dance now?' he said.

Ionna smiled, took his hand and let him lead her on to the dance floor.

Taking her in his arms, they began to slow dance to the traditional romantic song.

Pressed against him, he was so tall, and his strength was evident. A mix of emotions warmed her heart and warned her heart.

She'd never slow danced with Leith like this before. They were perfectly in tune. Maybe they always had been and she'd never seen him in a true light for the shadow of Roary. What if she had? The thought jarred her. What if she hadn't left the village to live in Edinburgh and had stayed? Would she have found the happiness that had always eluded her?

Dancing with Leith to such a beautiful song affected her in so many ways, but she swept aside thoughts of becoming romantically involved with him. It would never work.

At first, Leith didn't say anything, and his silent strength reminded her of the past. The man able to say so much with silence.

Part of him felt happy to be dancing with Ionna, but now he had to decide whether to risk taking things further, or not.

They danced on, and she felt him pull her closer as the song rose to a romantic crescendo.

As the song finished, their lips were a breath away from touching. Leith resisted the temptation to kiss her, and released her from his arms.

'Thank you for the dance, Ionna.'

Glancing outside, Leith quickly excused himself.

Striding over to the patio doors, he gazed out at the night sky. When he'd been outside talking to Roary, he'd sensed a storm in the air. Unable to shake off the feeling that a storm was on its way, he stepped outside and heard a rumble of thunder. The lively music had started up again, and no one heard it over the popular song.

Leith hurried over to Brochan. 'I think there's a storm coming,' he confided, stepping up on to the stage to tell him without causing a fuss.

Donal joined them. 'Storm clouds are scudding over the sea.'

Brochan turned the music down. 'Sorry to cut short your evening, folks, but there's a storm on the way. If you want to head home before you get drookit, you should go. We have regular ceilidh nights, so we'll hold another one soon. But it's been a great night anyway.'

Thanking Brochan and Bhictoria for the fun evening, everyone started heading out. The storm was rolling in across the sea, whipping up the waves. The waves rarely swept up from the shore, but the local community liked to make sure they were home, sheltering from the rain. When the summer arrived early, merging with the spring, storms like this sometimes happened.

The crafting bee ladies left in a group and most of them stayed in cottages near each other. Ionna and Effy were with them, then they took a slightly different route along from Leith's cottage, exposed to the full blast of the gusts sweeping up from the shore. Effy's cardigan was buttoned up, and they linked arms with each other, hugging close as they headed home.

Leith came running after them. 'I'll make sure you get home safe.'

'We'll be fine,' Ionna said as a gust of wind nearly blew her dress up.

'Come on,' he said, shielding them against the wind.

'Thank you, Leith,' said Effy, grateful for his concern.

'The storm will have blown past by the morning,' he assured them.

Their cottage wasn't far from the hub, and they were there in a few minutes, windblown but safe.

Leith walked them up to the cottage door and waited until they were both inside.

Waving, he walked away.

Ionna peered out the door window watching him trying to keep his kilt down.

Effy looked over her shoulder and giggled. And then he disappeared into the stormy shadows.

'Do you want a cup of tea before you go to your bed?' Effy offered.

'Yes, it's been quite a night.'

Effy had left a lamp on in the living room, and by the cosy glow they went through to the kitchen and Effy started to make the tea.

'Did you find out what Roary and Leith were talking about?' said Effy.

'No, did you hear any gossip?'

'Not a peep, but there are few secrets in this village. We'll find out soon, though I'm betting they were talking about you.'

'What a topsy–turvy night.' Ionna flopped down on a kitchen chair and sighed wearily.

'Did the laird invite you to have dinner with him? Go on a date?'

'No, I didn't encourage him. I sort of did the opposite.'

'I bet that was a new experience for Roary.'

Ionna nodded thoughtfully. The evening had been a new experience for her too. Having feelings for Leith. Feelings that could only end in heartache. He would never want to move to Edinburgh, and she had no plans to stay in the village.

CHAPTER THIRTEEN

'The flowers have perked up after the rain,' Ionna called through to Effy. After breakfast, Ionna stepped outside into the back garden to check the flowers, leaving the kitchen door open. Sunlight shone in a bright blue sky the next morning, erasing any hint of the previous night's storm.

Effy looked out the living room window as she packed the embroidery kits for the orders that had come in overnight. Cutting pieces of white cotton fabric to size, selecting the various colours of threads needed for the patterns, the needles, a hoop, and the patterns with instructions, she had a makeshift little assembly line set up on her work table.

'It's going to be another warm, sunny day,' Effy called back to her.

Ionna crouched down and took close–up pictures of the yellow and orange marigolds glistening with the last droplets of water before the sun dried them. Her photography was interrupted by a call from her editor, Lucy.

'Morning Lucy.'

'All your designs for the patterns have been approved.' Lucy updated her on the details of the morning's publishing meeting. 'So we want you to push on with the new floral designs.'

'I will. I'm planning to work on more of them today.'

'But we'd like you to make videos showing you working on your embroidery,' Lucy told her.

'Highlight how you do the various stitches and your techniques, including crewelwork, needle painting, whitework and goldwork embroidery. We want you to put them on your website, and we'll use them for promoting the new book.' Lucy explained the details.

'Okay, I'll do that,' said Ionna, wondering how she'd create these. She didn't put videos up on her website. She didn't even know how to edit them. But surely she could learn. Several of the crafting bee ladies, although not Effy, made these types of videos for their websites.

'Thank you, Ionna. Keep me updated. Speak soon,' said Lucy.

Ionna went through to the living room and told Effy about Lucy's request.

'I'm sure you can manage those. Lots of folk put videos up on their websites. I just haven't needed to do this yet, but it's something I would consider for myself,' said Effy. 'Ailish, Mairead, Vaila and others use their phones to film themselves crafting.'

'Lucy says they've had feedback from book customers wanting to see my embroidery techniques. And they want me to include a video of myself outside your cottage to tie–in with the embroidery pattern that will be on the cover of the book. Add a bit of context and interest.'

Effy smiled. 'I'll help you all I can, and I'm sure Ailish and the others will teach you how to edit the videos.'

Ionna sighed heavily. 'I don't want to encroach on their time. They're all busy with their crafting businesses. No, I'll figure something out. It can't be that hard.'

Effy understood, but planned to tell the ladies, knowing they'd rally round if Ionna got stuck. She continued to make up the embroidery kits ready for posting later.

Ionna tucked her sketch pad and pencils in her bag. 'I'm heading out to take pictures of flowers that I want to include in the book.' She wore the shift dress and put her phone in her pocket. 'The flowers in your garden weathered the rain, but just in case there are more storms coming, I want to take the photos while the flowers are looking pretty.'

Knowing that Leith would be at Ailish's cottage discussing fabric, Ionna headed to his cottage to take pictures of the forget–me–nots and foxgloves she'd seen in his garden.

The sea breeze wafted up from the shore, and she breathed in the fresh morning air as she approached Leith's cottage. He didn't appear to be home, and she planned to use the gate this time. No clambering over the bramble hedging.

Leith put the two poached eggs he'd cooked on to the two split muffins on his plate. He'd woken up after the ceilidh night with a keen appetite and was in the middle of making himself a tasty breakfast when he saw Ionna in his back garden.

Having taken the pictures she wanted in the front garden, she'd wandered round to explore the flowers outside his kitchen.

So intent in capturing close–ups of the blue asters she'd found, she didn't notice him peering at her out the window until he knocked on the glass and startled her.

He was in! She didn't want to look like she was deliberately trying to gain his attention after their *almost kiss* last night at the ceilidh. She was sure he'd wanted to kiss her when they'd finished their waltz, and she couldn't entirely say she would've resisted. Nothing but trouble would've come from giving in to his firm lips, but trouble tended to be part of her world.

Smiling tightly, she gave him a cheery wave, tucked her phone in her pocket and made as casual a bolt as she could for the nearest hedge to exit his property before he came out and confronted her.

Too late. Leith was quick off his mark, and opened the kitchen door before she could escape. He wore jeans and a clean white shirt with the sleeves rolled up to the elbows, revealing the whipcord muscles of his forearms.

'What's the rush?' He called to her. 'Come back. You're welcome to photograph any flowers you want. I told you that.'

'I thought you'd be out. I didn't want to disturb you.'

'Ailish realised later last night that she was due a delivery of new fabric this afternoon, including prints she thought I'd like for the cottages. I'm popping round in the afternoon.'

'I didn't realise you'd changed your plans,' she said.

He stood in the kitchen doorway, his broad shoulders and fit build almost filling it. 'I'm making a cooked breakfast.'

'I had tea and toast early this morning.' She'd always enjoyed the early summer mornings when she'd lived at the village. Effy was an early riser, and Ionna had been up since first light too and rustled up tea and toast for the two of them.

Leith waved her inside.

'Come in. I'll give you a muffin.'

Ionna went inside and hung her bag on the back of a chair. The kitchen table was set for one, but he put a plate and cutlery down for her to join him.

She looked at the two poached egg muffins. He transferred one on to her plate and gestured for her to sit down while he made the tea.

'No, you were going to have a hearty breakfast,' she said. 'You don't need to half it with me. A cup of tea will be fine.'

Leith brushed aside her concerns.

'Help yourself to tomato, brown or fruity sauce from the cupboard,' he said, pouring two mugs of tea and adding the milk.

She went over and selected the tomato sauce. 'What do you want?'

'Just salt and pepper.' The cruet set was on the table.

Smiling to herself, she lifted the sauce and sat down opposite him, preparing to add a dollop to her egg. 'You trust me with a bottle of tomato sauce when you're wearing a clean white shirt?'

He sprinkled his egg with salt and a dash of pepper. 'I'll take my chances. Unless you're determined to get the shirt off my back.'

No mishaps as she added the sauce and put the bottle aside.

'How did your phone call go with your editor?' he said as he ate his breakfast.

'Great. And Lucy phoned me this morning to say that all my patterns so far have been approved. But...they want me to make short videos demonstrating my embroidery.'

'That sounds reasonable. I'm sure people will enjoy seeing your skills.'

Ionna elaborated on what Lucy had said. 'They want me to put them on my website.'

'You should, and add a new photo of yourself.'

She realised he'd been looking at her website. 'I don't like having my photograph taken.'

'I can't imagine why not,' he said. 'You're the most beautiful woman I've ever met.'

A blush started to form across her cheeks and she took a sip of her tea.

'The thing is,' she began. 'I don't know how to edit the videos. Effy says Ailish, Mairead or other ladies from the crafting bee will teach me, but I'm not here to take up their time. I've already caused enough trouble.'

'Video editing?' he wanted to clarify.

'Yes. I think I can film myself stitching an embroidery, but it'll need edited to make it suitable for the website.'

'I can do that for you.' He sounded confident.

'Really?'

'I do video editing for all my clients,' he explained. 'That's how I present my architectural drawings for the building work. It lets them see what I have in mind watching the videos.'

Ionna hadn't considered this would be part of his business. This could solve her problem without foisting the extra work on to the crafting bee ladies.

'That would be handy,' she said, grateful for his help. 'Once I get back to Edinburgh I'll take a class in how to do it myself. But with the book's deadline...I'd like to take you up on your offer.'

'That's settled then.' He continued eating his breakfast.

Ionna tucked into hers. 'I'll make a plan of what stitches and techniques I'll demonstrate and then I'll use my phone to film those and give you a copy to edit.'

Leith nodded, but added another suggestion. 'I'll film you embroidering outdoors in the sunshine, show the beauty of the Scottish Highlands, the sea, the forest, Effy's cottage garden. But for the videos you make on your own indoors, you'll need proper lighting, lamps set up on your desk or table.'

Ionna liked his ideas. 'I'm using a table by the window in Effy's living room. I'll find out what type of lighting I need. Ailish and the others will know, and I'll order them.'

'Come with me to talk to Ailish this afternoon. I don't know anything about fabric. Maybe you could help me decide on the fabric for the curtains, quilts and other things.'

'Yes, I'd be happy to help you.'

'She gave me fabric swatches.' He reached across to the samples on the kitchen dresser beside the paint charts and lifted them over.

Ionna looked at the various designs. 'The floral prints are pretty, and you could pick out colours to suit the paintwork.'

'Ailish and a few other ladies from the crafting bee are going to make everything once I decide on the fabrics. I don't want them to have to rush to finish everything on time, so I'd like to select them this afternoon.'

Ionna lifted the paint charts over and held them up, gauging the tones in the fabric swatches. Seeing how the colours could be made to pop. 'I love this pink rose print fabric. It's a classic design, and the greenery creates a nice effect.' She looked at the icky cream on the paint chart and didn't comment, but wondered if it could be offset by the light cream background of the pink rose fabric.

'I'll have a look at Ailish's lighting set–up for her videos while I'm there, and order something similar for what you need,' he said.

'I don't want you to be out of pocket,' she said. 'I'll pay for whatever is ordered.'

'Let me buy the order,' he insisted. 'For old times' sake.'

'There were no old times for us.' A slight sadness sounded in her comment.

His broad shoulders shrugged this away. 'There could've been.'

She smiled at him, feeling her heart ache a little.

176

'Let me buy the order as a late birthday present for you,' he said. 'Six years worth. I think I'm getting a bargain.'

Ionna laughed and relented. 'Okay, thank you.'

They finished their breakfast and he cleared away the dishes while Ionna went out into his back garden to photograph more flowers.

He watched her through the window, wishing things could've been different in the past, wishing they could be now, but knowing she was leaving after the summer and going back to Edinburgh.

But he was determined to help her with anything he could while she was here, and become the gentleman he wanted to be. And at least, her trusted friend. A summer of fun and friendship with Ionna. He'd settle for that. She'd surely break his heart again when she left. But he'd rather endure that than an empty heart. He'd always loved her. He always would.

CHAPTER FOURTEEN

'Do you have any of your embroidery with you?' Leith said to Ionna. He stepped out of the kitchen into the sunny garden.

Ionna stopped taking pictures of the flowers and glanced over at him. 'I've always got embroidery in my bag.' At least one project in a hoop, usually two or three, depending on what patterns she was working on. 'Why?'

Leith looked up at the bright blue sky. 'It's a lovely day. If you wanted, I could film you doing a bit of your embroidery so we could see what works for you.'

Ionna liked his idea and went into the kitchen where her quilted tote bag was still hanging on the back of a chair.

'I've been embroidering a goldwork bumblebee. And a pansy pattern.' She showed him the two embroideries in the hoops. Threads were tucked into two small bags, separating each project, along with her needle book.

She'd made the needle book herself from fabric, quilted hexies, wadding, ribbon trim and soft felt. Flowers and butterflies were embroidered on the front of it. A small pair of scissors slotted into one of the pockets inside the needle book, along with a little measuring tape, other bits and bobs, and a variety of needles secured in the felt.

'Let's film your bumble.'

Ionna laughed.

'The gold thread will sparkle in the sunlight,' he said.

They went outside into the garden where he had a wooden bench he'd made for relaxing and enjoying the sea view.

Ionna sat down and started to set up her embroidery — making sure the fabric was taut in the hoop, threaded a needle with a single strand of gold metallic thread, secured the thread in the back of the work, and brought the needle up through the fabric ready to stitch the next part of the bee.

'How should we do this?' She'd watched enough online videos to know roughly what she'd do, but wanted his suggestions. He seemed to know what he was doing as he held up his phone and framed her ready for filming.

His heart ached, seeing her sitting there, a natural beauty, her hair like spun gold in the sunlight, with the backdrop of the colourful flowers in his garden. The perfect setting for filming her embroidering a bumblebee.

'Paint me a verbal picture,' he said. 'Tell me where you are and what you're doing. I'll film you from here so people can see you. Then I'll move in for the close–ups of you embroidering the bee so they can see the stitches.'

'What if I stumble over my words? Can you edit those out?'

'Yes, I can easily edit the video. I just think you should have at least one video of you talking to the camera. In other videos I can record you separately while you sew, and then add the voiceover.'

'You sound like an expert on this,' she complimented him.

'I've been making videos for the building work for years. I just don't put mine online.'

'I know. I couldn't even find a picture of you,' she inadvertently admitted.

Leith smiled broadly. 'So you were checking up on me when you were in Edinburgh?'

'I happened to be looking at Ailish and Mairead's websites, and I was just curious to see what had happened to you. What you looked like now. What had become of you.' She tried to make light of this. 'We used to be friends, of sorts.'

'We were friends,' he clarified. 'We still are.' Even though his heart was still broken and there was no patch on the near horizon that would mend it.

'I imagined you'd have made a success of your building business. You were always building and working on something.' She toyed with the gold thread, twisting it around the needle. 'And settled down, married. You were the marrying kind.'

Her words took him aback, and his heart jolted, realising she understood him better than he'd thought.

She unwound the thread and let slip a comment. 'But certainly not the fit and handsome man you've turned out to be.'

Leith's reaction made her try to rewind the compliment.

'What I mean is...I thought you'd be more mature and worn around the edges from all the hard building work.'

'I'll take the compliment.' He stepped nearer, peering through the camera, making sure he'd have the close–up shots in focus. 'So, you think I'm fit and handsome?'

'And cheeky!' She blushed and tried not to smile.

He laughed as he stepped back to begin the video for the wide shots.

'And chatty!' She threw another smiling accusation at him. 'You used to be the strong, silent type.'

'I learned that keeping my lips buttoned backfired more often than not.'

Those firm, highly kissable lips that were smirking at her right now.

'Let's begin...' He pressed record on his phone.

Flustered, thinking about kissing him, then forcing herself not to think about kissing him, she dropped her needle and had to pick it up.

'Keep going,' he instructed. 'I'll edit out the fumbles.'

'Fumbles and bumbles,' she retorted, smoothing the thread, ready to stitch.

'I might keep that comment in,' he teased her.

Ionna smiled right at the camera. The perfect picture of her. A genuine smile, sitting in the summer sunshine. Doing what she'd always loved — embroidering, and being playfully annoyed with him.

'This is a bumblebee goldwork pattern,' Ionna began. 'I'm using a single strand of gold metallic thread. I've stitched part of the body, creating the textured effect with long and short stitches.'

Leith moved in for the close–ups of the glistening gold thread being worked on the body of the bee. She stitched for a couple of minutes, filling in part of the design.

Ionna nodded to Leith, indicating that she was moving on to demonstrate another technique. She changed her thread.

'Now I'll show you how I embroider the wings using trellis stitch. As you can see, I'm bringing the thread up at the edge of the wing, taking it diagonally across to the other side and down through the fabric. Then I repeat this across the whole wing, creating an openwork trellis effect.' She changed her thread again to a dark gold tone. 'To hold the trellis work secure, I then make small couching stitches across several part of the trellis design where the threads intersect.'

Leith was fascinated to see how she did this.

Nodding to him that she was about to conclude the video, she held the bee up so that it shone in the sunlight, tilting it back and forth to show the glistening effect.

'For my goldwork, I include gold effect beads, sequins and wires in some of my patterns.'

And she was done.

Leith clicked the video off.

Ionna took a deep breath. 'How was that?'

'If it's as perfect as I think, it'll be almost ready to go.' He held the phone so she could watch what he'd filmed.

She stood close to him, eager to see how it had come out.

'You've filmed this so steady,' she exclaimed. 'And look at the gold thread sparkling in the light. This is great.'

'Great work,' he said, giving her the credit. 'Those were some finicky stitches.'

'I'm used to it, but I'll buy clamps to hold my embroidery hoop and the phone when I'm working inside at my table. It'll let me have both hands free to embroider without putting the hoop down or wobbling.' She smiled up at him. 'Or I should say, you'll buy them. Part of my six–year birthday bargain bundle.'

He laughed. 'Add whatever you want to the order.'

'Could I order a cup of tea? I kept holding my breath, trying not to fouter or fumble my words.'

'Tea coming right up.' Leith strode into the kitchen and she heard him fill the kettle.

Sometimes his willingness to accommodate whatever she wanted touched her heart so deep.

Sipping her tea, she sat in the living room beside Leith at his desk while he showed her how easy it was for him to edit the video on his laptop.

Walking through from the kitchen into the living room, she'd noticed the yucky pale green tins of paint in the hallway and made no comment. 'Those are for painting the hall,' he'd said, seeing the disapproval in her expression.

But she certainly approved of his video editing.

Cutting it down to around five minutes, the video was ready shortly after she'd finished her tea. 'This is excellent. Thank you, Leith. I'm going to send this to Lucy to let her see it.'

'You're an expert at embroidery. And it shows.' Again he gave the credit to Ionna.

Sitting close to him, she felt comfortable in his company.

Then she noticed her three embroidery books on his desk underneath a folder. She picked them up. Unlike the copies Roary had in his library, these books looked well read. 'You have my books!'

'Yes.'

'Did Effy give you these copies?'

'No. I bought them each time one came out.'

Ionna's smile lit up her face. 'I didn't know you were a fan of embroidery,' she teased him.

'I'm not. I'm a fan of the woman who embroidered the patterns.'

She smiled to herself and put the books down again on his desk.

'Can I make a suggestion?' he said.

'Yes.'

'You're going to include a video of Effy's cottage. We could do that this morning, before lunch, while the flowers are still blooming as they were in your pictures.'

Ionna stood up immediately. 'The video would match the pattern! It would show that I designed it from the actual cottage and garden in the summer.'

Leith towered over her as usual as he stood up too. 'I'll make a video like the one we've just filmed.'

'Let's go!' she said, picking up her bag.

'Hang on, I'll take the fabric swatches and paint colour charts with me to save me coming back for them.' He put them in a large folder that he used for the paperwork and plans. 'We'll go from there to Ailish's cottage.'

Striding ahead of him, Ionna walked through the hall, making no snippy comments on the yucky pale green on the tins of paint.

'I know you don't approve,' he said as they headed out.

'I didn't say anything about the yucky green.'

He laughed as she gave him a mischievous smile.

'It's your cottage, Leith. I'd just have opted for a light eau–de–nil.'

Chatting about home decor colours, they walked down to Effy's cottage.

Effy piled up her customer orders on the hall table ready for delivery in the afternoon. The aroma of the hearty pot of soup boiling made her go through to the kitchen and give it a stir. It was ready. Made with lots of fresh vegetables and lentils, it would be an easy lunch served with slices of bread.

'I've brought trouble with me, Effy,' Ionna called out as they walked into the hall.

Effy scurried through, wondering who it was, and then joined in the joke. 'Oh, it's you Leith. I almost didn't recognise you with your shirt on.'

Leith held his hands up. 'I'm outnumbered. I give in.'

Ionna explained what they were planning.

'A video of you and the cottage!' Effy exclaimed excitedly.

'Yes,' said Ionna. 'I'll get the embroidery ready.' She hurried through to the living room where she had her material on the table at the window.

Leith followed her through while Effy went back into the kitchen.

Ionna put a piece of white cotton fabric in a hoop, and started to draw the pattern on to the fabric.

'Do you want me to film this?' Leith offered. 'There's plenty of light shining in the window.'

Ionna nodded and began to describe her method of tracing the pattern on to the fabric ready for embroidering.

When she finished and had the hoop ready, along with the threads in her sewing box, they went outside to the front of the cottage where Leith set up a small garden table and chair from the back garden.

'Before you sit down to embroider, stand beside the cottage so I can capture this first,' said Leith.

Ionna suddenly had an idea. 'I want to take my dress off!'

'Fine by me,' Leith said jokingly.

'No, I'd like to wear the new dress Effy made for me. I'll be right back.' Ionna ran into her bedroom, took the shift dress off, put the floral wrap dress on, ran back out and stood in front of the cottage.

'You look great,' he said, and began filming.

'This is my Aunt Effy's cottage in a Scottish Highlands village on the west coast beside the sea,' she began. 'And this is a new dress that Effy made for me. She taught me how to embroider, quilt, sew, knit and other crafts when I was a wee girl. Effy holds

186

embroidery bee nights in her cottage, attended by the ladies of the local crafting bee.'

Leith nodded, encouraging her to continue.

'I've designed a pattern based on the cottage and the flowers from the garden for my new embroidery book.'

He filmed her as she walked over and sat down to begin the embroidery, moving in for the close–ups as he'd done for the bumblebee.

She demonstrated how she stitched various parts of the cottage, showing a few stitches so that snippets of everything were included.

'The roof is satin stitched using crewel wool to create a textured effect,' she said.

Leith was fascinated to see how she made the tiny bees flitting through the lavender. And the way she expertly created French knots.

She concluded by embroidering part of the flowers. 'I use lazy daisy stitches to create the tiny petals on the flowers.'

Smiling, she held up the embroidery in the hoop while Leith moved slowly back for a full shot of the scene with the cottage in the background.

'Perfect,' he said, finishing filming. He showed her part of the footage. 'This will work. I'll edit each piece to fit nicely together.'

'Oh, look!' Ionna exclaimed. 'Effy's caught peeking out the living room window in that shot. Just for a second.'

'I can edit that out if you want.'

'No, keep it in,' Ionna insisted.

Leith agreed. 'It adds a wee personal touch.'

They were so busy looking at Leith's phone, that they didn't notice the man walking towards the cottage. He wore dark trousers, an expensive shirt and waistcoat, dressed to impress, looking like class and money.

The tall, confident figure of Roary halted when he saw Ionna in the front garden laughing and chatting happily with Leith.

Roary had slept on his decision whether to continue to pursue Ionna, and had come to invite her to have dinner with him later at the castle. But the cheery scene he was watching made him change his mind.

Without either of them seeing he'd been there, the laird headed back towards the forest and his castle, leaving the past where it belonged, where it had ended so long ago.

CHAPTER FIFTEEN

'Do you want to stay for lunch, Leith?' Effy called out to him from the cottage's front door. 'I've made a pot of soup.'

He glanced at Ionna, and she nodded, encouraging him.

'Yes, I'll carry the table and chair round to the back garden.'

While he did this, Ionna filmed him in front of the cottage. 'Smile, Leith,' she said.

His sexy smile lit up her heart as he gave her a wave. He wouldn't be in the embroidery video, but she'd captured a memory of him for her personal archives. Something to look back on to make her smile when she went home to Edinburgh, and the warm summer in the Highlands was a distant memory.

Ionna, Leith and Effy sat at the kitchen table having their lunch, enjoying the soup, and then tea and shortbread. The door was open and the warm air wafted in.

'If there's time before we go to discuss the fabrics with Ailish, could you come and see the other two cottages I'm working on?' Leith said to Ionna.

'Yes, I'm interested in seeing them.'

'It would give you a look at the interiors so you can help select the fabrics,' he added.

'Ailish always has a lovely range of fabrics for her quilting,' said Effy. 'You'll be spoiled for choice.'

'That's why I'm keen to have Ionna's input,' he said.

189

Finishing their tea and shortbread, Leith and Ionna walked to one of the cottages nearby.

'In my building plans, and for the sake of clarity, I call this cottage two, and cottage one has the extension,' he said. 'Then there's my cottage.'

Ionna nodded that she understood.

Leith showed her around cottage two. 'I'm aiming to finish the exterior building work soon. I don't want to be disturbing the whole village throughout the summer. The exterior of this cottage is nearly done. And I've been decorating some of the rooms.'

Ionna smiled to herself when she saw that he'd painted the living room and the two bedrooms icky cream.

'I know what you're thinking, Ionna.'

She smiled tightly. 'It's a nice cottage, and the cream decor looks fine.'

'I've still to paint the kitchen to match,' he told her.

She tried not to smirk.

'But the hall is going to be this colour.' He opened the folder and showed her the burgundy colour on a paint chart.

Digging deep to find something positive to say, she gave him her opinion. 'I prefer the burgundy rather than the...green tone you're planning for your own cottage.' She glanced around. 'What colour will you paint the hall ceiling?'

'All the ceilings will be soft cream.' He pointed to the colour on the chart.

She forced herself not to guffaw.

Leith started to smile. 'Go on, laugh.'

She giggled, and then stepped back and viewed the cottage objectively. 'The cream and burgundy will be classy. It's a traditional cottage. We'll pick fabrics that will enhance this style.'

He tapped the folder he'd brought with him. 'I've got all the window measurements for the curtains, and other details that Ailish told me to bring.'

Ionna commented on the living room. 'This will be cosy in the evenings, especially when the curtains are up.'

He appreciated her comments. Then he checked the time. 'I'll show you cottage one. I'm still working on the extension's flooring, but the main structure is done and the glaziers have put the windows in.'

They walked to the next cottage and Ionna's face lit up with a smile when she peered into the spacious living room where the extension was built. 'I like this. It's bright and airy. Are you going to repaint the walls?' They were the light white she'd suggested to him for his cottage.

'No, I've painted them. Now I've only the special flooring to install. I painted the walls first because I don't want to risk any paint splashes on the beautiful floor. I won't mess the walls when I lay the flooring down.'

She went to go in for a better look around, but his hand clasped hers. 'Careful where you step. I've done some work already on the floor.'

Holding his hand, she leaned in to look at the extension. 'The new owner of this cottage is going to have a wonderful view of the sea.'

191

'The large windows will need curtains. I'm going to install the rails and I'd welcome any ideas you have for this.'

'I know what I'd have if this was my cottage,' she said, knowing it had already been sold. 'A modern classic floral print. Light cream background with colourful flowers such as roses, cornflowers, daisies and forget–me–nots. Pretty flowers.'

'I like the sound of that,' he said. 'The furniture for the cottages is already bought and in storage. Couches and chairs, dining tables, beds. I'll kit the kitchens out, installing new cupboards and dressers, depending on what the buyers listed they wanted. It was all included in the purchase cost.'

'Walk–in ready.'

'Exactly.'

'What a wonderful feeling it must be to walk into a beautiful cottage that's furnished and ready to settle in.' There was a wistful tone in her voice. She pictured having to find a flat for herself in Edinburgh at the end of the summer. A tense frown formed on her brow.

'Something wrong?'

'No, just thinking about...stuff.' She didn't elaborate and eased back into the hall, letting go of his hand and wandered through to the kitchen.

'It's basic,' he said, following her. 'I haven't installed anything yet. But...here's a peek at the plans.' He showed her the architectural video on his phone.

'Wow! Your video really brings the whole concept to life. I'm impressed. No wonder you're so skilled at making my embroidery videos.'

A message came through on his phone. He read it. 'Ailish is home with the new delivery of fabric. We should go.'

He locked the front door and they headed out to Ailish's cottage.

Ailish smiled when she saw that Ionna was with him, knowing this would make it easier to select the fabrics.

Leith opened the folder and handed Ailish the list of measurements.

'I've just had a whirlwind tour of the cottages,' Ionna told Ailish.

'Great, I've laid out the fabric samples on my work tables,' she said to Ionna and then smiled at Leith. 'My quilting has sort of taken over the house. The living room is a quilter's paradise. It is to me anyway.'

'I'd love to have an entire craft room for my embroidery. I had to use a corner of my living room in Edinburgh,' Ionna said to Ailish.

Ailish smiled and gestured around. 'I seem to have quilting in the whole house. Even the kitchen. The old–fashioned dresser is filled with part of my fabric stash.'

'Effy has her fabric stash in the living room,' said Ionna. 'Since I moved back, I've added my embroidery. But it feels like home. We had a coorie in craft day and it was great fun.'

Ailish led them over to the work tables. 'I've divided the cottages and fabric samples into three sets. Leith's cottage, and cottages one and two.'

Leith brought the fabric swatches out of the folder. 'I've had a look at the fabric samples you gave me, Ailish, but I'd welcome both of your suggestions.'

They started to look through the new fabric that had just arrived.

'This design looks like the one you described that would be ideal for the windows of the extension,' Leith said to Ionna.

Ionna agreed with him. 'The windows are large,' she told Ailish. 'I thought a print like this would suit them.'

'I've ordered plenty of this fabric.' Ailish checked the list of measurements. 'Yes, I have enough to make curtains and other bits and pieces, like cushions, if you want them to match. Or the quilt for the back of the couch.'

'Maybe match the curtains and cushions,' said Leith. 'But make the quilt different.'

'I could make a patchwork quilt with these fabrics.' Ailish lifted up a pre–cut bundle of fabric that was a mix of florals and solid colours. 'The light florals and pastels would tone well with the curtains and cushions.'

'That sounds ideal,' he said. 'What do you think, Ionna?'

'This would work with the colour scheme and the light and airy feeling of the living room,' said Ionna. Then she noticed some other swatches of prints that had butterflies and dragonflies in the floral designs. 'I like this collection. These would be lovely for the bedrooms, varying the designs for each room, but keeping them in the same colour spectrum.'

194

Ailish agreed.

Leith was happy for their expertise in mixing and matching the fabrics, combining patterns and solid colours. Within an hour, they'd selected all the fabrics.

'I appreciate your help with this, Ailish,' said Leith. 'And to you too, Ionna.'

'I'll make a start on getting the fabrics cut for each cottage,' said Ailish. 'A few of the crafting bee ladies have agreed to help with the quilting and sewing. We'll have everything done well ahead of your schedule,' she assured Leith.

'Before we go, could I see what type of lights you use when you're making the quilting videos for your website?' Leith said to Ailish and explained why.

Ailish was delighted to show them her set up. 'I have two lamps that I can adjust depending on the light I need for the video. And an adjustable phone holder so that I can work hands–free while I'm filming my quilting. It's nothing too fancy or complicated, and it suits me fine.'

'This would work for my embroidery videos,' Ionna said, sounding sure she could work with this. 'Leith is going to edit the videos.'

He took a note of the items and where Ailish had bought them. 'I'll order these and have them delivered soon,' he told Ionna.

Thanking Ailish for her help, they left and he walked Ionna back to Effy's cottage.

'Do you want to come in for a cup of tea before you go home?' Ionna offered.

'Yes, I'll look up the items online and it would be handy if you were there to confirm these,' he said.

'It's us, Effy,' Ionna called out, then she noticed the parcels were gone from the hall table and Effy wasn't at home. 'She'll be at the post office with her parcels,' she said to Leith. 'Come through while I make the tea.'

Leith sat in the kitchen and started to order the items while the kettle boiled.

'Thankfully, everything is in stock and will be delivered soon.' He clicked his phone off and relaxed back in his chair as Ionna put two cups of tea down on the kitchen table. She opened the back door to let the warm, late afternoon air pour in.

'I hope you didn't think I was interfering when I suggested the fabrics for your cottage,' she said.

'The designs you picked for the curtains, cushions and quilts looked great to me and if you think they'll brighten the icky cream and yucky green, that's a bonus,' he said, teasing her.

'Don't make me feel bad,' she said. 'I already feel bad enough for...' She sipped her tea to wash away her comment.

'What?' he said.

Ionna took a deep breath. 'For making bad decisions in the past.'

'We both did.'

'Mine were loads worse than yours.' Throwing herself at the laird was one of them. She still cringed with embarrassment.

'No arguments from me.'

She swiped at him playfully, and as he raised his hand to pretend to defend himself from being skelped,

196

their fingers brushed against each other and she felt a spark charge between them.

Leith felt it too. 'You're a wee firecracker,' he joked, blowing on his fingertips.

Ionna playfully made a sizzling sound.

Effy overheard as she walked in from the back garden instead of using the front door.

'Och! It's just you pair of eejits acting like cheeky bairns. I thought there was a snake in my kitchen,' Effy said, joining in the fun. 'Did you get all your fabric sorted out?'

'We did,' said Ionna. 'And Leith gave me a tour of his other cottages. I was fair impressed.'

'Ailish advised us on what to buy for setting up the lighting for Ionna's embroidery videos,' he said. 'I've ordered what we need. The items will be delivered to the wee shop.'

'Jinnet's just told me when I was in the shop,' said Effy. 'She'll keep a lookout for your orders.' Effy unpacked the groceries she'd brought from the shop. 'Are you staying for dinner with us, Leith? I'm making mince and tatties.'

'No, I don't want to impose,' he said, standing up to leave.

Effy looked at him. 'That's the thing about having pale blue eyes like yours. I can see when you're telling fibs.'

Leith smiled at her.

'Away through to the living room the pair of you and I'll rustle up the dinner.' Effy shooed them out of the kitchen.

Laughing, they went through to the living room and Ionna went over to her table at the window. Her sketchpad was open where she'd been designing a pattern.

'When the items arrive, we'll video you sketching your designs, showing the artwork for your patterns.'

'Okay.'

He picked up and looked at the mechanical pencil she used to start all her designs, then the fine art black ink pens she used for the final artwork.

'The new table lights will be handy for when I'm sketching on dull days,' she said.

Leith gazed out the window at the gorgeous sky and glistening sea. 'I don't think there will be many of them. So let's make the most of the sunny days while you're here. Just friends.'

Ionna nodded.

Over the next few days, Ionna made progress with her embroidery patterns, and Leith worked hard on the three cottages.

The equipment for making the videos arrived on time, and Leith helped to set it up for Ionna. To try out the lighting and phone clamp set–up, he helped her film her bee garden embroidery.

Giving her the thumbs up that everything was set, she began by holding up the finished embroidery in the hoop and talking about the different parts of the pattern.

'My bee garden embroidery pattern includes little satin stitched bee hives. To create the effect of tiny bees buzzing around the hives, I've used two shades of embroidery thread, dark brown and golden yellow, and a scattering of seed stitches. The foxgloves, cornflowers and bluebells are all embroidered with satin stitch and back stitch for the stems.'

It was a short video clip, but worked well.

'Can I do another quick one?' Ionna said to Leith, picking up another embroidery in a hoop that comprised of a row of small flowers.

Leith nodded and Ionna moved seamlessly into the next video.

'Border designs are great for embroidering along the edges of cushions and tablecloths. This is my wildflower patch — a row of pretty flowers.' She gestured to each flower on the close–ups. 'There's a wild rose, thistle, poppy, Cupid's dart, foxgloves, sunflowers, daisies and Queen Anne's lace.'

Leith rolled his hand, indicating that she should keep going. She had several embroideries in hoops within easy reach, and these were the sort of short clips that could be added easily to her website.

'I often embroider motifs on to my clothes to add a personal design to tops, skirts, jeans or jackets. Motifs are also handy to hide a repair or cover a blemish on vintage clothes I've bought. These are some of my floral motif patterns. Orange blossom flowers, iris, pansy, night scented stock, and coral bells. And butterfly, bee and dragonfly motifs.'

Ionna nodded that she was finished and Leith stopped the filming, showing her how to do it herself.

She bit her lip. 'I've just given you three videos to edit.'

'These are easy.'

'How is your building work going?'

'Making progress. But I'm thinking of having a night off instead of painting walls. I'm slightly ahead of schedule. Someone has spurred me on. I've even painted the hall in my cottage. And yes, I used the green. It looks okay.'

'Once the carpet is down it'll feel cosy.'

'No carpet, just the polished wood flooring.'

'Ah.'

'It'll be easier to keep clean from muddy boots coming in and out from the garden,' he reasoned.

Winding herself up, she let rip. 'If it was my cottage, I wouldn't let anyone traipse through my clean hall with mucky boots on!'

He tried not to laugh.

Realising she'd overstepped, she rewound her remark. 'Not that it has, or ever will, have anything to do with me.'

'Seeing as you're in a feisty mood, do you fancy going swimming?'

'With you?'

'No, on your own. I'll relax on a deck chair on the sand and watch you tackle the waves while I have a cup of tea and a sandwich.'

'Very funny.'

It was the late afternoon, merging into the early evening, but the sun was still shining gold and sunny across the glistening turquoise sea.

'I'll put my swimsuit on and grab a towel,' she said.

Wearing the blue chambray dress over her swimsuit, and carrying her towel in bag, she walked with Leith up to his cottage so he could get changed into his trunks. The afternoon gave way to the early evening, and a burnished glow shone over the coast, but there was still heat in the fading sun.

The cottage's front and back doors and windows were open wide.

'I'm airing the cottage while the paint dries. Wait here,' he said, indicating that she should wait in the garden.

'The smell of paint won't bother me,' she said, keen for a nosy at the decor.

'I don't want you sticking to the walls.'

Doing as she was bid, she stood in the garden while he hurried in to put his trunks on.

Memories of those trunks hiding very little the night he'd emerged from the sea flickered through her thoughts. She was still trying not to think about him looking fit when he came back out.

'That was fast.'

He wore jeans over his trunks and a pair of canvas shoes, and clasped a rolled up towel.

'It doesn't take me long to get my clothes off. Especially when you're around.' Bold and bare–chested, he smiled at her.

They started to walk down to the shore.

'As you're in a fun mood, let me remind you of something,' she said. 'I recently beat you at running. Remember, I used to swim faster than you too.'

'You always cheated,' he said, accusingly.

'You told me there were no rules when we swam along the coast.'

'Well, no rules this evening, Ionna.' There was smirking determination in his tone.

'Fine.'

They walked down on to the sand, kicking their shoes off. Several people were in swimming, but they were scattered around the dunes area, so they had no one to interrupt their coastal challenge.

The sand felt warm and soothing on the soles of her feet, and the dazzling sparkles off the surface of the water looked like they were about to swim in a sea sprinkled with diamonds.

Maybe in a way, she was, Ionna thought, because her life had become enriched since she'd come back here.

Ionna took her dress off.

The colour of her turquoise swimsuit matched the sea.

'Wearing a camouflage cossie won't work,' he joked. 'I'll still see you floundering when we race along the coast. I swim here regularly, especially in the evenings.' He eased the broad muscles in his shoulders. 'It works off the tension from a long day's building work.'

Ionna stretched her slender arms out and limbered up. 'I've had a hard day of embroidering a goldfinch, an owl and a crewelwork robin. Hundreds of long and short stitches, and redesigning my robin's wonky beak. So, I'm in barracuda mode.' 'There are no barracuda in this sea,' he told her.

'There will be tonight,' she said flicking her ponytail. 'Don't be a grumpy loser.'

Ionna sprinted into the sea, making him play catch up, and dived under the water.

'Why you wee...' he muttered, laughing, diving into the sea and powering after her.

The crafting bee ladies had arrived at Effy's cottage for their embroidery bee night.

Settling themselves down and helping Effy make the tea and set up the cakes, they wondered where Ionna was.

'Is Ionna not here for the embroidery bee?' said Jinnet.

'No, she's away swimming in the sea with Leith. They'll be racing each other. Ionna loved the sea,' Effy reminisced. 'She used to go missing for hours when she was a wee girl. I sometimes thought she was lost in the forest. But I always found her playing down the shore.'

'The pair of them are becoming really close–knit,' Mairead commented.

Effy agreed with a heavy sigh. 'Both their worlds will unravel when she has to go back to Edinburgh.'

Leith swam beside Ionna.

'You're keeping up well,' she called over to him. 'Race you back to the shore.' She dived below the surface, disappearing, turning around under the water and then emerging and swimming fast, determined to leave him floundering in her wake.

Catching him off guard again, he found himself enjoying the challenge, and her company. He loved her sense of adventure. But he wasn't going to let her win without swimming hard and fast to beat her to the finishing line. It used to be when they were level with his cottage.

Ionna swam full out, knowing that Leith would be on her tail. No glancing back to see how close he was. Only a quick look for the finishing line — Leith's cottage. Nearly there. Unless Leith was submerged sneakily to claim a surprise win, tonight's trophy was within seconds of her grasp.

Finishing, she stood up, and swept her wet ponytail back from her face.

Leith was a few seconds behind her, then he stood up and walked towards her, smiling.

'You win, this time,' he conceded.

'Oh, so you think we'll be swimming again?'

'There's a lot of summer left.'

Ionna picked up her dress and wrapped her towel around her shoulders.

Leith lifted his towel but held it in his hand, exposing his lean physique dripping wet with sea water.

Was he tempting her? No, she didn't think so. He was just a walking temptation.

'Would you like to get cleaned up at my cottage?' he offered.

'The embroidery bee is on tonight at Effy's cottage. I'd like to go and join in the tail end of it.' Then she thought that she'd shower anyway before joining in the bee. So she accepted Leith's offer, hoping to nosy at the decor. 'But, okay. A quick shower at your cottage. I promise I won't stick to the walls.'

Grinning, he walked with her to his cottage. She headed straight to the bathroom, took her swimsuit off and stepped into the shower.

'There are clean towels in the bathroom dresser if you need them,' he called through to her, pouring himself a refreshing glass of cold water in the kitchen.

'Thanks,' she called back, showering hurriedly, trying not to feel that the bathroom walls would look so much nicer if he'd painted them a light shade of aqua rather than the grey blue tone.

Stepping out, clean and refreshed, she used one of the towels from the dresser to dry herself. Her own towel had sand on it. Towel drying her hair, she brushed it smooth. Then she put her dress on, stepped into her pumps, left his towel in the bathroom and walked out with her own towel rolled up.

'I don't like to dash, but there's an hour left of the embroidery bee,' she said, feeling herself react to seeing him standing in his kitchen wearing only his trunks.

'Go, it's fine. I'm going to jump in the shower. Thanks for coming for a swim.'

'Thanks for not being grumpy.' She didn't mention the word loser. Leith was nothing like that.

He walked her out, and she made no comment about the green walls in the hallway.

'Enjoy your embroidery bee. And send me the video clips. I'll edit them tonight.'

Waving, she smiled at him. 'I will.'

Leith stood at the door watching her walk away. One day, she'd be walking away again, leaving like she did before. His heart felt torn every time he thought about them parting. But he'd no intention of curtailing their fun this summer while she was with him.

'Did you win?' Effy said to Ionna when she walked in to join the embroidery bee.

'Yes, but Leith was very gallant, and I had a shower at his cottage before coming here.'

Effy guffawed. 'So Leith's the one that got the clothes off you this time.'

Ionna blushed and smiled. 'Nothing scandalous happened.'

'That's a pity,' Mairead joked. 'We're short on gossip this evening.'

'Then let's talk about embroidery,' Ionna suggested, settling down to join in the bee.

A light shone from one of the turrets of the castle. Then it went out, throwing the upper levels into darkness, while the lower level, especially the front entrance, was all aglow.

Roary hurried down the stairs, elegantly dressed in a suit, shirt and tie and carrying a black briefcase filled with a small fortune in paperwork for the business deals he'd secured.

Highlighted against the dark backdrop of the trees in the forest, he put the briefcase in the boot of his expensive black car. It was already filled with three suitcases ready for his business trips to the cities.

Donal and Gorden stood backlit by the lights in the front entrance to wave him off. The running of the castle and the estate was in their hands until he came home in the autumn.

Roary started up the car, revving the powerful engine, and with an acknowledging nod to Donal and Gorden as they waved to him, he drove off into the night, through the depths of the forest.

CHAPTER SIXTEEN

The ladies were helping Effy make another round of tea and cakes when a message came through on her phone.

Effy put the slice of carrot cake down that she was serving, and read it. 'Donal says that Roary has left the castle tonight. It's a business trip.'

'When will he be back?' said Bhictoria.

'Autumn.' Effy looked at Ionna. Not with accusation, but for her reaction.

'I'll have left the village by then,' Ionna said, knowing that the ladies surmised she was the reason he was leaving.

Another message came through from Donal.

'Donal says it's a lucrative business trip to a few cities, including Edinburgh, Glasgow and London.'

Effy messaged her thanks to Donal.

'We'll find out more details soon,' said Ailish.

'But he'll miss the next ceilidh,' Bhictoria said, sounding disappointed. 'Brochan and I hoped the laird would start to frequent the hub.'

'Ach, we'll probably enjoy it all the more without the drama he brought with him the last time,' said Effy.

The other ladies agreed.

'When is the next ceilidh?' Ionna said to Bhictoria.

'Two nights from now. The storm curtailed the last one, and Brochan wants to reschedule another one to fit in with our other party nights.'

'Are we all going?' Jinnet said cheerily.

They all agreed that they'd go.

'Maybe you should tell Leith to get his kilt and sporran ready,' Effy said to Ionna.

'Maybe I will.' Ionna smiled and lifted a tray of tea through to the living room to continue their embroidery bee.

The following morning, Ionna sat at her table and prepared to finish working on one of her embroidery patterns — needle painting a blue butterfly in three shades of blue using long and short stitches to fill in the wings. She'd finished most of it the previous night during the embroidery bee.

From the window, she saw Effy outside at the garden gate talking to Donal. He'd picked up a parcel for her at the wee shop and was dropping it off to her as he went by. The window was open, letting the sea air waft in, and Ionna could hear their conversation.

'Any more news about the laird?' Effy said to Donal.

'He drove to the Cairngorms and is staying there for a few days.' The laird liked to go to the Cairngorms, a beautiful part of the Scottish Highlands. 'Then he's driving to one of the cities on his itinerary, and starting the rounds of his business dealings in various cities. He's staying for two or three weeks in each one. Roary is like his father. His business trips are always lucrative.'

'I thought he was home for the summer,' said Effy. 'He wasn't long back from his business away.'

'Aye, and I know folk will gossip and assume he's run away while Ionna is here, but I think it is business.

Roary keeps all his private business paperwork secure in one of the castle's turrets. He was up there last night, collecting his briefcase before he left. Though perhaps it's ideal timing for him to leave.'

'I think so,' Effy agreed.

'I've heard that Ionna and Leith are spending a lot of time together.'

'They are, and he's already mended my shoogly shelf in the kitchen for me without prompting.'

'Leith's a good man,' said Donal. 'I'd just hope his heart isn't put through the mincer again when Ionna leaves the village.'

'I worry for her too,' Effy confided. 'She was a shadow of herself when she arrived, and now she's perked up. The spark between the two of them is obvious. But it can only ever be a summer romance.'

'Grab happiness while you can, I always say. Speaking of which...I hope you'll be up for a dance with me at the ceilidh.'

'I will. Ionna and I are planning to have our dinner there again before the dancing.'

'See you on the dance floor, Effy,' Donal said chirpily, and walked away giving her a wave.

Effy brought her parcel inside and opened it in the living room. 'My new thread has arrived. Donal dropped it off.' She looked eager to see the colours. 'But he says there's no more gossip about the laird.'

'I heard,' said Ionna, glancing at the open window.

Effy sighed and put the thread delivery down. 'I hope you don't think I was being snippy about you and Leith.'

'I don't. You're right. So is Donal. I'm grabbing a happy summer while I can with Leith, with you, with the crafting bee ladies, and I'm looking forward to dinner at the hub and the ceilidh.'

Effy smiled. 'Bhictoria said last night that Brochan has a special lunch menu this week. Do you fancy having lunch at the hub with me today? My treat this time.'

'You're on!'

Effy picked up the new threads again, and while Ionna continued embroidering the butterfly, they chatted about the new colours and textures of the thread and crewel wool.

'We're spoiled for choice again,' Ionna said to Effy, studying the delicious items on the lunch menu. They sat at a table in the heart of the hub. It was fairly busy, and Bhictoria came over smiling to take their order.

'We're flummoxed for what to have,' Effy said to Bhictoria.

'I can recommend Brochan's pizza. He bakes his own scrumptious bases and the toppings are generous. The mixed red, yellow and orange peppers, red onion and courgette with herbs and spices is my favourite.'

Ionna closed her menu. 'That sounds delicious. I'll have that.'

'So will I,' said Effy.

'It's served with a crisp green salad,' Bhictoria added with a smile.

While they ate their lunch, they chatted about crafting...and romance.

Ionna cut into her pizza. 'Is there anything going on between you and Donal?'

Effy spluttered into her tea and started blushing. 'No!'

'You're blushing, Effy.'

'It's the spices and the hot day.'

'I like Donal,' said Ionna. 'He's always cheery and kind. It's just that...I think that he'd take your friendship further with a wee bit of encouragement.'

'Probably he would,' Effy admitted. 'But we're both happy dancing at the ceilidhs here, partnering up for the Christmas and New Year balls at the castle. And during one of the game nights at the hub, he enticed me to join him for a couple of games of dominoes.'

'Did you win?'

Effy giggled. 'No, I was always chapping.'

Ionna smiled, pleased that her aunt had so much fun at the village.

When they finished their pizza, Ionna ordered summer pudding and Effy opted for the chocolate trifle. Their conversation continued to focus on romance.

'Are you going to encourage Leith to come to the ceilidh?' said Effy. 'Not that I think he'll need much encouragement.'

'I'll tell him we're going and let him decide if he's up for another ceilidh night.' She thought that he would be, and so did Effy.

'At least we know for sure that Roary won't come striding in to cause ructions,' said Effy.

'Now that Roary's away, I'd like to pop up to the forest and make a video while the pink bluebells are blooming. I didn't want to risk running into Roary again under the current circumstances. But now I'm free to wander in the forest. I thought I'd ask Leith to film me. I won't need many more videos on my website, but I'd like one featuring the forest.'

'Your publishers seem happy with your videos,' Effy commented.

'They are. Lucy says they plan to use your cottage video to start promoting the new book.'

Brochan came swaggering over with four fancy cocktails on a tray. 'I necd lassies to taste test my new concoctions.'

Effy gestured to a busy table near the window. 'I'm sure they'll be happy to help you.'

Brochan put the tray down on their table. 'Take a wee sip of them and tell me how they taste.' He placed a champagne flute down in front of Effy. 'This one is a variation on your sherry cocktail, with extra fizz. An effervescent Effy.'

Effy laughed and took a sip. 'Jings! It's full of bubbles.'

'A special sparkling champagne cocktail,' Brochan confided.

Effy held on to the glass. 'Champagne? Perfect for a celebration cocktail.'

'Are you celebrating something, Effy?' Brochan said, sounding interested.

Effy lifted up the cocktail again. 'No, but I'll think of something once I've finished this.'

Brochan laughed, and then turned his focus to Ionna. 'Try a sip of this one. It's not potent. Nice and refreshing on a hot summer's day. An icy Ionna.'

The ice tinkled in the tall glass as Ionna picked it up and took a sip of the sparkling spritzer. 'Really refreshing. Great for the summer.'

'Next up, Effy, try this.' Brochan gestured to the lavishly decorated with fruit cocktail.

Effy expected it to taste of fruit, and was surprised when the other flavours kicked in. 'Is this whisky? Brandy? Rum or cognac?'

Brochan grinned. 'Yes.'

Effy smiled.

'And finally...' Brochan offered up a white cocktail topped with whipped cream and cherries.

Ionna thought it looked like it was made with vanilla ice cream and lemonade with cream on top.

Ionna sipped it and ended up with cream on her nose.

The laughter from their table created interest from the other diners, and Brochan found himself having to whip up cocktails for them too.

Leith had taken it upon himself to sort Effy's front garden gate while he had his tools with him as he went by on its way to his own cottage. He wore jeans and an open neck sky blue shirt with the sleeves rolled up. It was a five–minute task to tighten the wobbly bolt.

He assumed Ionna and Effy would be in the living room, sitting out the back door, or maybe Ionna was on one of her adventures to wherever there were flowers, butterflies, birds and other things to sketch for her patterns.

But he realised he was wrong as he secured the lock on the gate and put his tools in his bag.

Two giggling figures walked towards the cottage from the main street.

'We're not tipsy,' Ionna said, seeing the smirk on Leith's face as they approached the cottage. 'We're just—'

'Full of fizz and cheeriness,' Effy cut–in.

'My cocktails were mainly ice cream, lemonade, fruity stuff and whipped cream,' said Ionna. 'With cherries on top.'

Leith suppressed his laughter. 'Were you pair of scallywags at the hub?'

'Effy treated me to lunch,' Ionna told him. 'We tried the new lunch menu. I had pizza and pudding.'

'And then Brochan needed our help to taste his cocktails,' Effy embellished.

Leith smiled at them. 'It seems you were very helpful.'

Effy straightened her cardigan. 'We were. One of my cocktails had champagne in it.'

Leith blinked. 'One of them? How many did you have?'

'Two each,' said Ionna. 'But sort of four as we shared our opinions of them.'

'So you had a mix of cocktails for lunch?' Leith summarised.

'Only four,' Effy emphasised. 'We're not ones for imbibing.'

'I can see that,' said Leith. 'Well, while you two were...helping Brochan, I mended the wobbly bolt on your gate.'

'That was very kind of you, Leith,' Effy told him.

Ionna eyed the closed gate and Leith recognised the mischievous glint in her eyes. 'When I was a wee girl, I used to take a run and jump over the gate into the garden instead of opening it.'

Effy nodded. 'So you did. You always had a lot of bounce in you.'

'I bet I could still do it.' Ionna stepped back as if she was lining up to have a go.

'Okay, ladies, that's it.' Leith opened the gate and escorted the pair of them into the cottage.

'Where's the coffee?' he called through to them as they sat and giggled in the living room.

'Leith thinks we're tipsy,' Effy whispered loudly to Ionna.

'We're tea jennies,' Ionna told him from her chair at the window.

He filled the kettle and put it on to make them strong cups of tea.

An urgent knock on the front door interrupted them.

Leith strode through to the hall and opened it to find Donal standing there looking anxious.

'Are the lassies okay?' Donal said to Leith. 'I was in the function room at the hub having a wee game of dominoes when Brochan told me he was concerned that they were tipsy. I said I'd check they got home safe without them causing trouble, especially Ionna.'

'Is that you, Donal?' Effy called through to him. 'Come away in. Leith's making tea.'

'There's no coffee,' Leith confided to Donal, and the two of them tried not to laugh.

'Aye, Effy, it's me.' Donal walked into the living room and smiled when he saw Effy sprawled comfy on the couch with her feet up. 'Your cheeks have a rosy glow to them, hen.'

'I caught the sun this morning in the garden when I was hanging out my washing,' said Effy.

'Aye, right,' Donal muttered, giving Leith a knowing glance. 'Brochan was worried about you.'

'Why?' said Effy.

'Because the pair of you danced out of the hub after your lunch,' Donal stated clearly.

Effy waved a dismissive hand in the air. 'Och, we were just practising for the ceilidh.'

Donal shook his head at Leith.

The kettle came to the boil.

'Would you like a cup of tea?' Leith said to Donal.

'Thanks, Leith.'

Ionna was sitting at her table holding up an embroidery she'd half finished, looking at it in the light shining through the window. 'I wanted to film a video of me stitching the pink bluebell pattern in the forest, in the midst of the bluebell patch. Maybe you'd help me do that this week, Leith.'

'I will,' Leith called through as he made the tea. 'Let me know when it suits you to go to the forest.'

Donal frowned. 'The pink bluebells took a battering with the storm. If it rains again they'll be past their best. You should go as soon as you can.'

Ionna perked up. 'Could we go now? The sun's out.' she said to Leith as he carried the tea tray through and sat it down on a table in the living room.

Leith looked at Donal.

'The wee pink flowers won't last,' Donal said to Leith.

'Drink your tea and then we'll go,' Leith told Ionna.

Ionna wore her floral print dress as she walked with Leith up to the forest. It was a short walk across the field and through the gap in the trees that led into the heart of the forest.

Donal stayed with Effy at her cottage having another cup of tea.

'The pink bluebell patch is over there.' Ionna led the way. She had her bag with the embroidery and thread that she needed. The tea and fresh air made her clear–headed and there were no lingering effects of the cocktail fiasco. She smiled, feeling excited about making the short video.

Bright afternoon sunlight filtered through the branches of the tall trees, casting a fairytale effect around her as she sat amid the flowers and set up her embroidery.

Leith remembered her wearing the dress the day she'd arrived, getting her car stuck in the mud. Events had gone full circle, and now here they were together in the forest, as friends for the summer.

He nodded that he was ready and held up his phone to capture the full scene of Ionna embroidering the flowers she was sitting in the heart of.

'I'm using two shades of pink thread to satin stitch the petals of these beautiful pink bluebells. They're in the forest that surrounds a magnificent castle in the Scottish Highlands.'

Leith nodded again, encouraging her to continue.

'I'm embroidering the outer petals with a light pink colour. And then using a deeper pink for the inside of the flowers.'

Leith moved in for the close–ups of the satin stitches, noticing that the light shining through the trees highlighted her embroidery.

'The stems are stitched with whipped running stitch using two strands of variegated green thread. The various tones of the green add light and shade to the greenery including the leaves. To fill in the leaves I'm using closed fly stitch. French knots are part of the pattern.'

Ionna continued to embroider for a few minutes, and then held up the hoop to show the pretty design.

She nodded to Leith that she'd finished, and he clicked the recording off.

Standing up, she came over to view the video on his phone.

His heart was pounding and he wondered if the adrenalin surging through him would be obvious to her. The effect her closeness had on him here in the forest. There was no one else around, and it felt as if they were sharing a magical time together that he wanted to keep and treasure forever.

The warmth of the summer, the shared seclusion, the intimacy between them...whatever it was, Ionna looked up at him. Her sweet lips smiled at Leith.

For the first time ever, he gave in to temptation and leaned down and kissed her, soft and gentle, and then as she responded, with passion and love in his heart.

Her softness melted into him, melting his heart.

And she felt the tender strength of his lean muscles pressing against her, claiming her, yet protecting her. She'd never kissed Leith before, though recently she'd imagined what it would feel like, and the reality exceeded all her dreams.

Suddenly, he pulled back and shook some sense into himself.

'I'm sorry. I shouldn't have done that. It won't happen again.'

Her lips and cheeks glowed with a rosy warmth from the effect of his kiss, and she blamed the romantic setting for dropping her guard. She'd been wanting him to kiss her. Now he had. And she hadn't resisted him. Standing there, she could still feel the burning passion from his lips on hers.

She shook her hair and tried to make light of what they'd given in to. 'We're both just out of sorts today, that's all. It's fine. We're friends still, just the way we were before.'

His heart thundered from frustration, mentally kicking himself for doing this, especially when she was so trusting, and he was supposed to be helping her with the embroidery video.

She walked back over to the pink flowers and gathered her things in her bag. 'Donal was right. Another round of rain and the pink bluebells will be gone.'

Just like Ionna would be at the end of the summer. Leith couldn't help that this thought shot into his mind. A dagger through his heart. But he hid it behind bravado.

'I'll edit this video tonight,' he said. 'And you can trust me.'

She smiled and nodded. 'I do. I always have. I always will.'

He went to leave the forest, but she brightened and gestured further into the trees. 'It's years since we were here together. And it's such a lovely afternoon. Let's take a walk up to the castle, just for a peek, and then come back down.'

He took no persuasion and carried her bag for her, offering his strong hand to steady her as they navigated parts of the gnarled tree roots.

'Can you use the timer on your phone to take a picture of us here in the forest?' she said.

'Yes.' He frowned. 'You want a picture of us?'

She shrugged. 'I don't have one. I barely have any of you. Set it up and take a picture for the archives, a happy memory to look back on some day.'

Leith tucked his phone into the branches of a tree, setting the timer as they stood together and smiled. His arm was around her shoulders.

The picture showed them close together, smiling, fooling the world that they were a happy ever after couple, when both of them knew this wasn't true. And in the current circumstances, never could be.

Emerging from an archway in the forest, they stopped and looked at the castle set in its own private gardens.

'Do you want to go over for a closer look?' he offered.

'No, this is fine.' There was a wistfulness in her voice. 'I just wanted a peek.' Nothing in her wanted anything more than to admire the historic beauty of the castle.

There was no sign of the laird. His car was gone. He'd left and he wouldn't be back until the summer, and Ionna, were long gone. And she was fine with this too.

'I always loved the architecture,' said Leith. 'The turrets spiralling into the sky, the solid structure of the castle, but with an elegance to the design.' The builder in him appreciated the castle's grandeur.

'It's a beautiful castle,' she said.

'Do you want me to take a picture of you with the castle in the background?' he offered.

'No, let's head back down,' she said with a gentle contentment in her tone, as if finally letting go of the last part of her own history with the castle and the laird, leaving it where it belonged, in her past.

Winding their way through the forest, they talked about their other plans for the summer.

'Do you sense a storm brewing?' she said as they navigated the gnarly route through the trees.

He breathed deeply. 'No, not a hint of it. The next few weeks are forecast to be scorching. I agree. There will be rain, drizzle sometimes, but I think the worst of the thunderstorms are by.'

'Great. I'd like to go swimming in the sea most days, work on my embroidery too. And in the evenings, go to ceilidh dances at the hub, Effy's embroidery bees, and the other ladies crafting bee nights.'

'We could go swimming tomorrow,' he suggested.

'We could go swimming tonight,' she said, sounding as if she was up for adventure.

'And then have dinner at my cottage,' he offered.

Ionna took Leith up on his offer.

Picking up her swimsuit from Effy's cottage, and smiling when she saw that Donal had stayed for dinner, Ionna went swimming in the sea with Leith in the early evening.

Two figures frolicked in the shimmering sea as the amber glow of the vast sky arching along the coastline became a deep bronze and copper sunset. The distant islands looked like they were floating on a dreamlike mist and then disappeared into the far horizon as the night sky started to twinkle with stars.

'Hungry?' he said as they sat on their towels watching the sea gently lap on to the shore.

'Yes.'

He stood up, reached down, clasped her hand and pulled her to her feet. 'Want to help me make dinner?'

'What's on the menu?'

'I restocked the fridge and freezer today from the wee shop. Tatties, veg, cottage pie, lots of things.'

They walked from the shore and headed to his cottage.

'Can I have a shower first?' she said.

'Yes, then I'll jump in after you and we'll rustle up a tasty dinner.'

'Swimming always gives me an appetite,' he said, having showered and put on dark trousers and a clean white shirt, unbuttoned at the neck, exposing a hint of his chest.

Ionna's hair was damp from the shower, but in the ambient heat she knew it would dry naturally.

Working together, they started making dinner.

Leith put a cottage pie in the oven while Ionna boiled up a pot of tatties.

He opened a tin of peas to go with their meal.

Ionna cut slices of crusty bread from the large farmhouse loaf and buttered them.

He finally made the tea.

She set the table.

He served up two plates with cottage pie, boiled tatties and peas.

She got the tomato sauce out of the cupboard. And the cruet set.

They sat down and smiled across the kitchen table at each other.

'I'm impressed,' he said. 'You didn't cause any trouble cooking dinner.'

'Ah, but the night is young...'

The night sparked in too fast for Leith's liking. How could it be almost midnight? They'd had dinner, washed the dishes, chatted, he'd edited the pink bluebell video and it was up on her website, she'd messaged Lucy to take a look, they'd discussed his building work on the cottages, they spoke about fabric and quilts, neither of them mentioned paint colour charts, and both of them had a great evening together.

'I'll walk you home, Cinderella.'

She picked up her bag and they headed out. One of the lamps was still on in the living room of Effy's cottage, but she'd gone to bed, leaving only the beacon of light on for Ionna.

They said goodnight at the front door.

'Are you going to the ceilidh night?' Ionna said to him.

'I am. Promise me a dance?'

'Promise.'

Smiling, Leith walked away, playfully jumping over the garden gate, causing Ionna to stifle her giggles so she didn't wake up Effy.

She watched him walk away, but before he disappeared into the shadows of the warm night, he turned and waved to her, as if he sensed she'd been watching him until he'd gone.

Ionna waved back to him, and then went inside, closed the door and fell asleep minutes after she snuggled up in bed.

Ionna continued to be busy with her embroidery work until the night of the ceilidh. Dinner at the hub included Leith. They'd invited him to join them for dinner before the dancing, and the three of them sat at a table near the window enjoying their meal. Ionna wore the white broderie anglaise dress, Effy chose a summery dress, and Leith had on his kilt, sporran and a white ghillie shirt that laced up the front. The laces were tied neatly and didn't reveal his chest, but again, the night was young, and a lively evening of ceilidh dancing was in store.

They'd recommended Brochan's lattice pie to Leith and he tucked into the puff pastry. Ionna had the Scottish cheddar salad served with thick–cut chips, while Effy wanted to try Brochan's savoury special with mashed potatoes and broccoli.

No cocktails for dinner, just tea for three.

They spoke about the items that the crafting bee ladies were making for Leith's cottages.

'We've scheduled the items between a few of us,' Effy said to Leith. 'Ailish is making the quilts, cutting all the fabric and piecing them. Some of us will help when needed if she gets busy with her other orders. But Ailish is such a fast and expert quilter.'

Leith had a mouthful of pastry and nodded at Effy as she continued.

'Mairead says she'll make the curtains for cottage one, including the large curtains for the extension. Vaila and a few others have divided out the other curtains and they'll have them sewn up between them. I'm making the cushion covers.'

'I'd be happy to help you, Effy,' Ionna offered.

Effy nipped that idea in the bud. 'Nope. You're here to work on finishing your book. There are plenty of us to sort out the sewing and quilting.'

Ionna nodded, knowing she was right.

'Besides, we all love to quilt and sew,' said Effy. And Leith was paying them well for their time and skill. So everyone was happy with the deal.

The ladies didn't mention to Leith about how much money he was making on the sales of the cottages, but everyone knew he'd already earned a substantial living from his years of building work. The sales of the cottages added to this and made him very comfortably off.

'Ailish said you repaired her cutting table for her this morning,' Effy said to Leith.

The broad shoulders beneath the ghillie shirt shrugged. 'She'd told me it wobbled when I was in talking to her about the fabric. I had my tool bag with me. It was a ten–minute task. But her table's sturdy again for cutting the fabric for the quilts.'

'Well, she was fair pleased,' Effy told him. 'And,' she emphasised, 'Jinnet told me you fixed the shelves in her wee shop.'

The shoulders shrugged off his good deeds. 'I was in for my shopping and Jinnet was standing on a step ladder trying to wedge spent matchsticks in the dookits to straighten the shelves. It was another ten–minute job, and she insisted on giving me a free ice lolly when I went in to buy a cold drink later.'

Ionna and Effy laughed.

'Sounds like a fair exchange to me,' said Ionna.

Brochan bounded by, smiling cheerily at them as he headed into the function room to set up the music for the ceilidh.

Several of the crafting bee ladies arrived early at the hub to settle in their seats, and then in walked Donal and Gorden and went up to the bar for their usual tipple of whisky.

'Here's your chocolate ice cream, lemon meringue pic and sticky toffee pudding,' Bhictoria said, serving up their puddings. 'And don't rush, you've time to enjoy your dinner before the ceilidh kicks off.'

Bhictoria hurried away to tend to other diners, and the restaurant was busier than the last time Ionna and Effy had been there for dinner. People from the small nearby town had turned up for dinner and dancing.

Ionna lifted her spoon and looked at the height of the meringue on her pie. 'Brochan has risen to the occasion again.'

Effy laughed, and then ate her chocolate ice cream.

Leith tucked into his sticky toffee pudding, and for a few moments, the conversation at the table went quiet as they all started eating the puddings.

Lively music sounded from the function room, and the lighting created a party atmosphere. Brochan had found a box of colourful balloons left over from the New Year celebrations, and had blown them up and hung them around the room, leaving a few spare for folk to have fun with.

Relaxing after their dinner, Ionna, Effy and Leith then heard Brochan gearing up to start the ceilidh. Leith escorted them through the busy throng to the function room in time for the opening announcement.

'Good evening, folks!' Brochan said with a broad smile. 'Welcome to the hub's ceilidh. Partner up for the first jig of the night.'

Donal nodded to Effy, and she went over to him. Gorden made a beeline for Jinnet. The crafting bee ladies found themselves partnered with crofters, farmers and men from the nearby town, leaving Leith standing beside Ionna.

Leith gazed down at her and smiled. 'You promised me a dance. And tonight, I'm going to hold you to it.'

He held out his hand and she accepted it, letting him lead her on to the dance floor. They joined in the opening jig, laughing at Effy and Donal as they skip–stepped by.

Everyone clapped when the jig finished, and Brochan kept the momentum going, leading straight into a fast–moving reel.

Ionna and Leith joined in, whirling around the floor, and then linked arms with friends, acquaintances and strangers as everyone danced and had fun together at the hub.

Brochan opened the patio doors to let the warm night air cool down the fervent revellers, and then swept Bhictoria on to the dance floor where he entertained everyone with an expert spurt of Highland dancing. Folk clapped in time to the music, and Brochan's nifty burling. And then he danced with his wife again.

Leith partnered with Ionna for most of the night, but also danced with Effy, Mairead, Bhictoria and other crafting bee ladies.

A rousing reel with all the men allowed Ionna and the ladies to stand at the edge of the dance floor and cheer their men on. The whirling was wild, and Leith threw himself into the thick of it, laughing and keeping up with the fast–moving dance. Brochan was in the midst of it, whipping up a storm with his leaps and twirls. All the men were kilted, and there were times when the laughter and cheers overpowered the music.

When the reel finished, Leith ran over to Ionna and clasped her hand. 'Come and get a breath of air, then we'll join in the dancing again.'

Smiling, Ionna let Leith lead them through the throng and outside into the calm night. There was barely a breeze wafting up from the shore, but the scent of the sea was refreshing.

'This is a great night,' said Leith, still holding her hand as he gazed up at the sky. The deep inky blue glittered with stars.

Ionna looked at Leith, committing the image to memory, her heart filled with joy.

He blinked out of his faraway thoughts and then gazed down at her. 'Are you having fun?'

'Lots of fun.' She smiled as she spoke. It was one of those nights when everything felt right, hopeful and happy.

'Promise me we'll have more nights like this,' he said, taking hold of her other hand, clasping both of them in his.

'I promise.'

Roars of laughter sounded from the function room, and when they looked in, Brochan had released a load of the balloons. A free–for–all of fun had erupted and they could see Effy swiping at one, trying to bounce it off of Donal.

Without having to agree, Leith and Ionna hurried inside to join in the melee before Brochan announced another lively reel.

The evening continued until a slow romantic waltz wound the ceilidh to a close.

'Shall we?' Leith said to Ionna.

She nodded, and let him take her in his arms and waltz to the romantic music.

It felt right to be in Leith's arms, she thought. Despite the summer's end on the far horizon, and the certainty of a broken heart, again, when it came time to leave the village for Edinburgh, she wouldn't give up the chance to enjoy herself with him. While it lasted. In her heart she was sure it would last forever.

As the last dance of the evening played, Leith pulled her close. The laces of his ghillie shirt had become undone earlier in the night from all the dancing. Not that she was complaining. The strong muscles in his chest made her heart beat. She could've blamed the lively dancing. But there was no point in lying to herself.

At the end of the ceilidh night, Donal bid goodnight, as usual, to Effy, and went on his way home. He'd had dinner with Effy at her cottage the other evening, but it wasn't the first time, and he was sure it wouldn't be the last. But they were friends. An easy friendship, easier to maintain than a romance.

Leith stuck to his promise not to overstep again, and after he walked Ionna and Effy back to their cottage, he waited until they were in safe and then waved as he walked away.

Over the next few weeks, the summer kept its promise of being a scorcher. And Leith and Ionna kept their promise to each other — to enjoy the summer together as friends, while they both tended to their work and responsibilities.

Swimming in the sea, sometimes in the mornings, during the day or in the evenings, was one of their regular pastimes together. Leith hadn't beaten Ionna at swimming yet. She was still faster than him. Maybe his heart was more concerned about protecting the love he had for her than exerting to win the races.

Her smiles were what he thought he'd remember the most when she'd gone. She thought the same about him. Neither of them revealed this to each other, keeping things as light and airy as the summer itself.

But one night, a storm did roar across the sea, darkening the atmosphere. Clouds blocked out the stars, creating a sky that looked like a watercolour in deep inky blues lit by bolts of lightning.

Leith had sensed it earlier in the day. The way the floral scent in his garden became stronger as the flowers readied themselves for the rain.

He'd completed all the building work on all three cottages. The interiors were decorated and furnished. Quilts, curtains and cushions added the finishing touches. But that was a few days ago. Everyone was a little ahead of schedule.

Leith had used his spare time wisely to wind down from the building work, and spend more time with Ionna. He'd even made a few more videos of her embroidery, filming in Effy's garden, amid wildflowers in a field and beside the sea. Her whitework lilies and lily–of–the–valley flower pattern was stitched entirely with white embroidery thread. He'd filmed her crewelwork robin design and colourful dragonfly.

But their time together was coming to an end.

The forecast was for a long, hot summer, extending well into the weeks after Ionna was due to leave for the city.

Unknown to Leith, she'd been thinking things over, wondering if she could work from the village instead of moving back to Edinburgh. After a lot of consideration, and knowing that she'd fallen in love with Leith, she made her decision lying in bed on that last stormy night, watching out the window, tucked up safe in bed.

Ionna had breakfast with Effy the next morning, but didn't tell her what she'd planned. She wanted to discuss this with Leith first, and walked up to his cottage.

The storm had blown by as usual, and the blue sky and sparkling turquoise sea looked like a lovely summer morning.

Leith was in his front garden when he saw Ionna walking towards his cottage, wearing a dress that matched the cornflowers.

He couldn't fathom her expression.

'Something wrong?' he said.

'I'd like to talk to you,' she began. There was no one nearby to hear their conversation.

Leith nodded, waiting for the dagger to his heart. Knowing she was leaving.

Ionna took a deep breath. 'I've decided I'm staying.'

He took this news in and then replied. 'I'm leaving.'

Her world tilted. 'You're leaving the village?'

'Yes,' he confirmed.

'When? Why?' She heard the panic in her voice.

'I'm packing the last of my things in the van today. Then I'm leaving in the morning.'

'I don't understand—'

'I've sold the cottages.'

'I know that,' she cut–in.

'All three of them. Cottages one and two, and my own cottage.'

'You've sold your cottage? But it's your home, you're grandfather's cottage. You were brought up here.'

'My grandfather wasn't. He was raised in a cottage far down the coast, almost as far south as the Isle of Skye. He didn't move up here until he got married. His father always advised him to make his own life, find a house for a new life. And my grandfather advised the same to me since I was a boy. I love this cottage, but I knew that one day, I'd find my own house somewhere else to start my own life, hopefully with the woman I wanted to marry. The latter part didn't pan out for me, but time was wearing on. So when I invested in buying the two cottages to sell, I decided to make it three cottages.'

'Why didn't you tell me you were planning to leave the village?'

'Because I was legally bound not to tell anyone.'

Ionna frowned. 'Why was it a secret? Everyone in the village knows the two cottages had been sold.'

'The buyer wanted it kept a secret. I sold cottage one as soon as I put it on the market. Then when I put cottage two and my own cottage up for sale with the estate agent that was handling things, a second buyer made a bid for cottage two and my cottage.'

'Someone bought cottage two and your cottage?'

'Yes,' he confirmed.

'Who was the buyer?'

'Roary.'

Ionna's world tilted further. 'Why does Roary want to buy two cottages? Especially your cottage?'

'To keep the properties in the community. He'll sell them to local residents when the time is right. Fortunately, I'd sold cottage one to someone with links to the village, so they're not an outsider. Roary said that whenever any of the cottages on the castle's estate become available, he's inundated with folk wanting to buy the properties and it causes a furore. The laird wants to avoid that. So he made the sales private. His lawyer and mine dealt with the paperwork, and I signed that I wouldn't reveal any of his plans to anyone in the village.'

Ionna started to understand why the laird wanted to ensure the cottages were kept for the community.

'As I told the laird the day you were due to arrive here, I wasn't changing my plans. And I haven't.' He shrugged off the weight that he felt on his shoulders. 'You kept telling me you were leaving and going back to Edinburgh.'

'I saw you talking to Roary outside the hub during the ceilidh night,' she said. 'You looked like you were arguing.'

'We were discussing business. Roary was concerned that I'd tell you our plans. I assured him I would not.'

'If you'd told me, I would've kept your secret.'

Leith's expression showed doubt.

Ionna relented. 'Okay, so maybe I wouldn't have. Unintentionally.'

'You're a troublemaker. And telling you could've led to more trouble. I signed the agreement. But more than that. I gave Roary my word. And that's binding. Besides, I agree with his intentions. It was a complicated situation, made even more tricky when we found out that you were coming back.'

Her heart was pounding, and the bright sunlight suddenly didn't seem so summery even though it shone as clear. 'Where are you going to go?'

Leith looked across at the distant islands, his favourite view from his cottage. 'Not too far. I've bought a cottage on one of the islands. Over the past while, I've renovated it. A traditional cottage, four bedrooms, an extension with a great view of the sea.' He dug his phone out of the pocket of his jeans and showed her a video of his new cottage.

Ionna stood close to him, wanting his arms around her for comfort from the shock of everything he was telling her. But she stood strong and viewed the video, blinking when she saw what he now owned.

'This is your new cottage!' she exclaimed.

'It is. And the decor has no icky cream or sludge colours. Those were Roary's choice, not mine, as he's used to the darker, traditional colours of the castle. My new cottage is bright and airy. The walls are white, light aqua in the bathroom, white and pastel yellow for the kitchen to make it look summery even on dull days. The hall is white. If you liked the colours in cottage one, I think you'll love the island cottage decor. And the large garden. It has two apple trees, flowers, a really pretty cottage garden.'

His video confirmed everything he said.

'This is the small town on the island. I've visited the island since I was a boy.' He showed her clips of the quaint main street lined with a selection of shops and businesses. A boat ferried people back and forth to the mainland. 'Folk are friendly and welcoming. And I'm booked up for building work on the island until this time next year.'

Ionna's world started to level itself. 'Well, congratulations on pulling off this fantastic deal and creating a dream cottage for yourself. I'm still going to stay here at Effy's cottage.' She sounded determined, but upset. Leith was leaving. He'd been the deciding factor in whether she stayed or went back to Edinburgh.

Needing time to think, to breathe, she started to walk away.

Leith watched her go and then called out to her. 'Come with me!'

Ionna stopped and looked round at him.

He walked towards her. 'I've always believed that we should be together. I've always loved you. I always will.' He moved closer. 'Marry me.'

Ionna's heart jolted and then soared with hope.

'Come with me to the island. It'll be a fresh start for both of us. I think that's what we need.'

Ionna felt all the love in her heart for Leith wash over her, and blinked away the happy tears that started to well up in her eyes as she looked at him.

Leith stepped closer still and gazed down at her. 'Be as adventurous as I know you are. Come with me to start a new life together.'

His hand gently brushed away the stray tears from her cheeks.

'I can't offer you a castle in the forest,' he said. 'But I can offer you a beautiful cottage on an island. Wasn't that always you're true fairytale?'

She started to nod and smile at him.

'You'll do it?' he said, wanting confirmation.

'I will.'

Leith took her in his arms and kissed the breath from her, and she returned his passion with all the love and adventure in her heart.

'I'll have to tell Effy,' she said breathlessly.

'Remember to tell her that once she's finished gadding about Scotland on her holidays, we expect her to come and visit us. And stay for weekends. We'll visit the village often too, and enjoy the ceilidh nights at the hub. It's only a boat trip across the water. Not too far.'

But far enough for their own life on the island.

Ionna kissed him. 'I'll tell her.' She hurried away, almost breaking into a run.

Leith watched her disappear into Effy's cottage, and moments later, Effy came out the front door and waved to him excitedly, both hands in the air. Yes, he thought with relief, Effy was happy for them.

A short time later, Ionna came running back up to Leith's cottage. 'Effy says we'll have a party in the hub the first time we're back here in the village.'

'I'm up for that,' Leith confirmed, while continuing to pack his belongings into the back of his van.

'Are you leaving your furniture?'

'Yes. I've got the island cottage all nicely furnished. Some new things, some stylish vintage pieces. You'll approve of those.'

'I'm sure I will.' Then she hesitated. 'Can I help you pack?'

'It's almost done. But we're leaving in the morning and driving to the nearby town to get the boat across to the island. I'll lead the way, and you follow me in your car. Don't get yourself lost.'

'I won't. And I promise I'm not going to cause any trouble from now on.'

Leith shook his head. 'I don't want you to change. I've always loved you as you are. Trouble, adventurous...'

She smiled at him.

'You should pack your belongings in your car,' he said, smirking. 'That should take you all of fifteen minutes.'

'Ideal for starting afresh. But I'll pack my video equipment, and the extra dresses I've been given.'

Leith leaned close and kissed her. 'Then come back and we'll spend our last night down the shore. Go for a swim. I'll let you win.'

'I always win.' Her heart reacted to his playfulness, but deep down she felt that she had finally found the happiness that had eluded her for so long. Coming home to the village led her to the true love of her life. The man who'd always loved her. And she'd always love him.

The night was a scorcher, as if the evening knew to put on its finest show of twinkling stars arching over the sea towards the islands.

Ionna and Leith swam along the coast, heading back to the finishing line, racing each other. Neither of them won as Leith playfully lifted her up and stood thigh–deep in the sea.

She squealed with delight as he threw her up and caught her in his strong arms and then carried her on to the shore.

They stood together, gazing out across the sea. His arms were wrapped around her, shielding her. 'See those wee lights shimmering far off on that island over there?'

The night air was so clear that she could. 'They look like fairy lights.' Her fairytale.

'That's home,' he said. 'Our home, Ionna.'

Leith pulled her close and kissed her. And she kissed him, looking forward to a happy life together on the island.

End

About the Author:

De-ann Black is a bestselling author, scriptwriter and former newspaper journalist. She has over 100 books published. Romance, thrillers, espionage novels, action adventure. And children's books (non-fiction rocket science books and children's fiction). She became an Amazon All-Star author in 2014 and 2015.

She previously worked as a full-time newspaper journalist for several years. She had her own weekly columns in the press. This included being a motoring correspondent where she got to test drive cars every week for the press for three years.

Before being asked to work for the press, De-ann worked in magazine editorial writing everything from fashion features to social news. She was the marketing editor of a glossy magazine.

She is also a professional artist and illustrator. Embroidery design, fabric design, dressmaking, sewing, knitting and fashion are part of her work.

Additionally, De-ann has always been interested in fitness, and was a fitness and bodybuilding champion, 100 metre runner and mountaineer. As a former N.A.B.B.A. Miss Scotland, she had a weekly fitness show on the radio that ran for over three years.

De-ann trained in Shukokai karate, boxing, kickboxing, Dayan Qigong and Jiu Jitsu. She is currently based in Scotland.

Her 16 colouring books are available in paperback, including her latest Summer Nature Colouring Book and Flower Nature Colouring Book.

Her latest embroidery pattern books include: Floral Garden Embroidery Patterns, Christmas & Winter Embroidery Patterns, Floral Spring Embroidery Patterns and Sea Theme Embroidery Patterns.

Website: Find out more at: www.de-annblack.com

Fabric, Wallpaper & Home Decor Collections:
De-ann's fabric designs and wallpaper collections, and home decor items, including her popular Scottish Garden Thistles patterns, are available from Spoonflower.
www.de-annblack.com/spoonflower

Also by De-ann Black (Romance, Action/Thrillers & Children's books). See her Amazon Author page or website for further details about her books, screenplays, illustrations, art, fabric designs and embroidery patterns.

Amazon Author page:
www.De-annBlack.com/Amazon

Romance books:

Scottish Loch Romance series:
1. Sewing & Mending Cottage
2. Scottish Loch Summer Romance
3. Sweet Music
4. Knitting Bee
5. Autumn Romance
6. Christmas Ballroom Dancing
7. Scottish Highlands New Year Ball
8. Crafting Bee

Music, Dance & Romance series:
1. The Sweetest Waltz
2. Knitting & Starlight
3. Ballroom Dancing Christmas Romance

Snow Bells Haven series:
1. Snow Bells Christmas
2. Snow Bells Wedding
3. Love & Lyrics

Scottish Highlands & Island Romance series:
1. Scottish Island Knitting Bee
2. Scottish Island Fairytale Castle
3. Vintage Dress Shop on the Island
4. Fairytale Christmas on the Island

Scottish Chateau, Colouring & Crafts series:
1. Christmas Cake Chateau
2. Colouring Book Cottage

Sewing, Crafts & Quilting series:
1. The Sewing Bee
2. The Sewing Shop
3. Knitting Cottage (Scottish Highland romance)
4. Scottish Highlands Christmas Wedding

Quilting Bee & Tea Shop series:
1. The Quilting Bee
2. The Tea Shop by the Sea
3. Embroidery Cottage
4. Knitting Shop by the Sea
5. Christmas Weddings

The Cure for Love Romance series:
1. The Cure for Love
2. The Cure for Love at Christmas

Cottages, Cakes & Crafts series:
1. The Flower Hunter's Cottage
2. The Sewing Bee by the Sea
3. The Beemaster's Cottage
4. The Chocolatier's Cottage
5. The Bookshop by the Seaside
6. The Dressmaker's Cottage

Sewing, Knitting & Baking series:
1. The Tea Shop
2. The Sewing Bee & Afternoon Tea
3. The Christmas Knitting Bee
4. Champagne Chic Lemonade Money
5. The Vintage Sewing & Knitting Bee

Tea Dress Shop series:
1. The Tea Dress Shop At Christmas
2. The Fairytale Tea Dress Shop In Edinburgh
3. The Vintage Tea Dress Shop In Summer

The Tea Shop & Tearoom series:
1. The Christmas Tea Shop & Bakery
2. The Christmas Chocolatier
3. The Chocolate Cake Shop in New York at Christmas
4. The Bakery by the Seaside
5. Shed in the City

Christmas Romance series:
1. Christmas Romance in Paris
2. Christmas Romance in Scotland

Oops! I'm the Paparazzi series:
1. Oops! I'm the Paparazzi
2. Oops! I'm Up To Mischief
3. Oops! I'm the Paparazzi, Again

The Bitch-Proof Suit series:
1. The Bitch-Proof Suit
2. The Bitch-Proof Romance
3. The Bitch-Proof Bride
4. The Bitch-Proof Wedding

Summer Sewing Bee
Heather Park: Regency Romance

Action/Thriller books:

Knight in Miami
Agency Agenda
Love Him Forever
Someone Worse

Electric Shadows
The Strife Of Riley
Shadows Of Murder
Cast a Dark Shadow

Children's books:

Faeriefied
Secondhand Spooks
Poison-Wynd

Wormhole Wynd
Science Fashion
School For Aliens

Colouring books:

Summer Nature
Flower Nature
Summer Garden
Spring Garden
Autumn Garden
Sea Dream
Festive Christmas
Christmas Garden
Christmas Theme

Flower Bee
Wild Garden
Faerie Garden Spring
Flower Hunter
Stargazer Space
Bee Garden
Scottish Garden
Seasons

Embroidery Design books:

Sea Theme Embroidery Patterns
Floral Garden Embroidery Patterns
Christmas & Winter Embroidery Patterns
Floral Spring Embroidery Patterns
Floral Nature Embroidery Designs
Scottish Garden Embroidery Designs

Printed in Great Britain
by Amazon